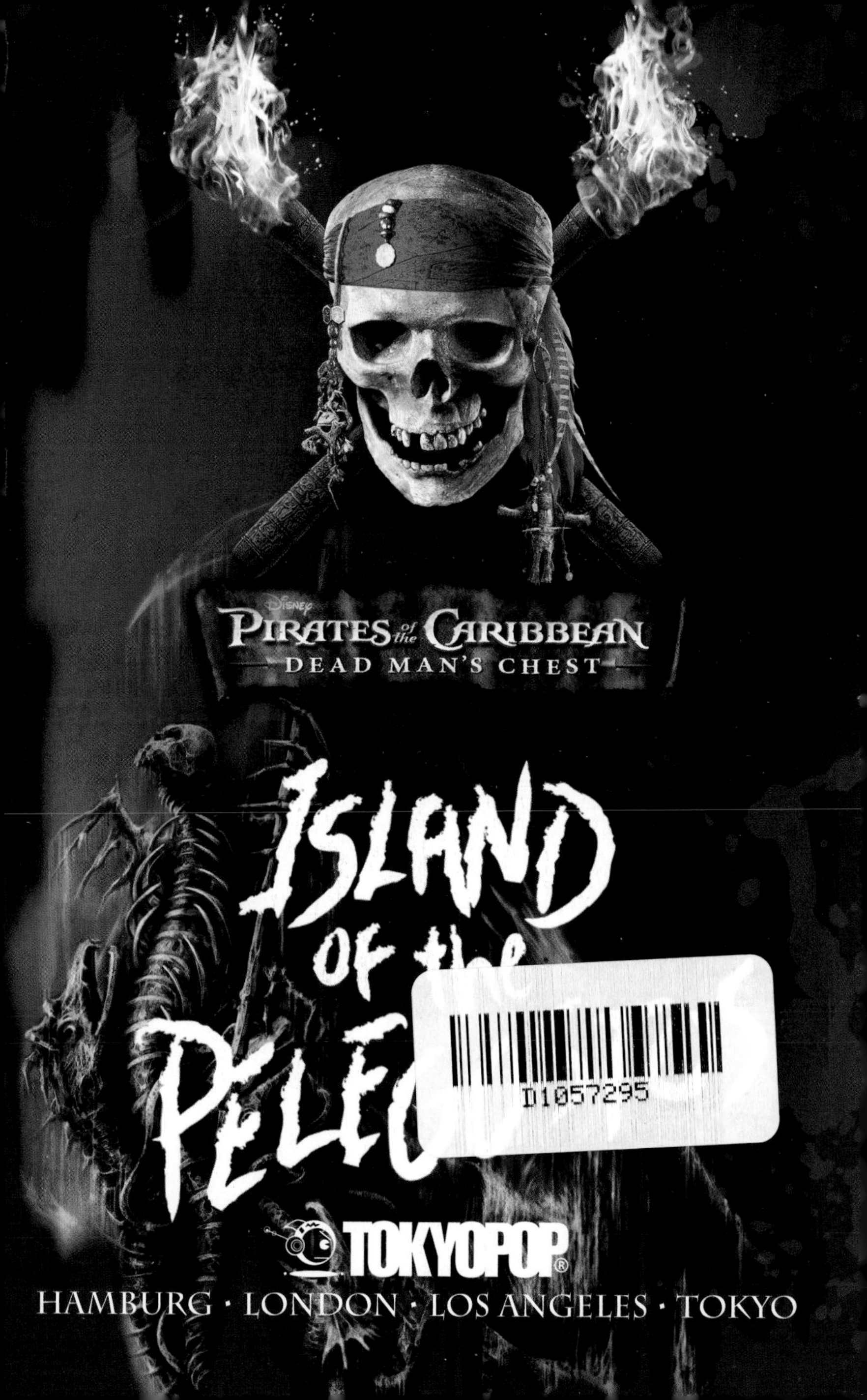
Disney
Pirates of the Caribbean
DEAD MAN'S CHEST
ISLAND
OF the
PELE
TOKYOPOP®
HAMBURG · LONDON · LOS ANGELES · TOKYO

Editor - Erin Stein
Graphic Designer, Letterer & Cover Designer - Tomás Montalvo-Lagos

Digital Imaging Manager - Chris Buford
Production Manager - Elisabeth Brizzi
Senior Designer - Gary Shum
Senior Editor - Elizabeth Hurchalla
Managing Editor - Lindsey Johnston
VP of Production - Ron Klamert
Publisher & Editor in Chief - Mike Kiley
President & C.O.O. - John Parker
C.E.O. - Stuart Levy

E-mail: info@TOKYOPOP.com
Come visit us online at www.TOKYOPOP.com

A **TOKYOPOP** Cine-Manga® Book
TOKYOPOP Inc.
5900 Wilshire Blvd., Suite 2000
Los Angeles, CA 90036

Pirates of the Caribbean: Dead Man's Chest
Island of the Pelegostos

Based on the screenplay written by Ted Elliott & Terry Rossio
Based on characters created by Ted Elliott & Terry Rossio and
Stuart Beattie & Jay Wolpert
Based on Walt Disney's Pirates of the Caribbean
Produced by Jerry Bruckheimer
Directed by Gore Verbinski

ISBN: 1-59816-482-1

First TOKYOPOP® printing: July 2006

10 9 8 7 6 5 4 3 2 1

Printed in the USA

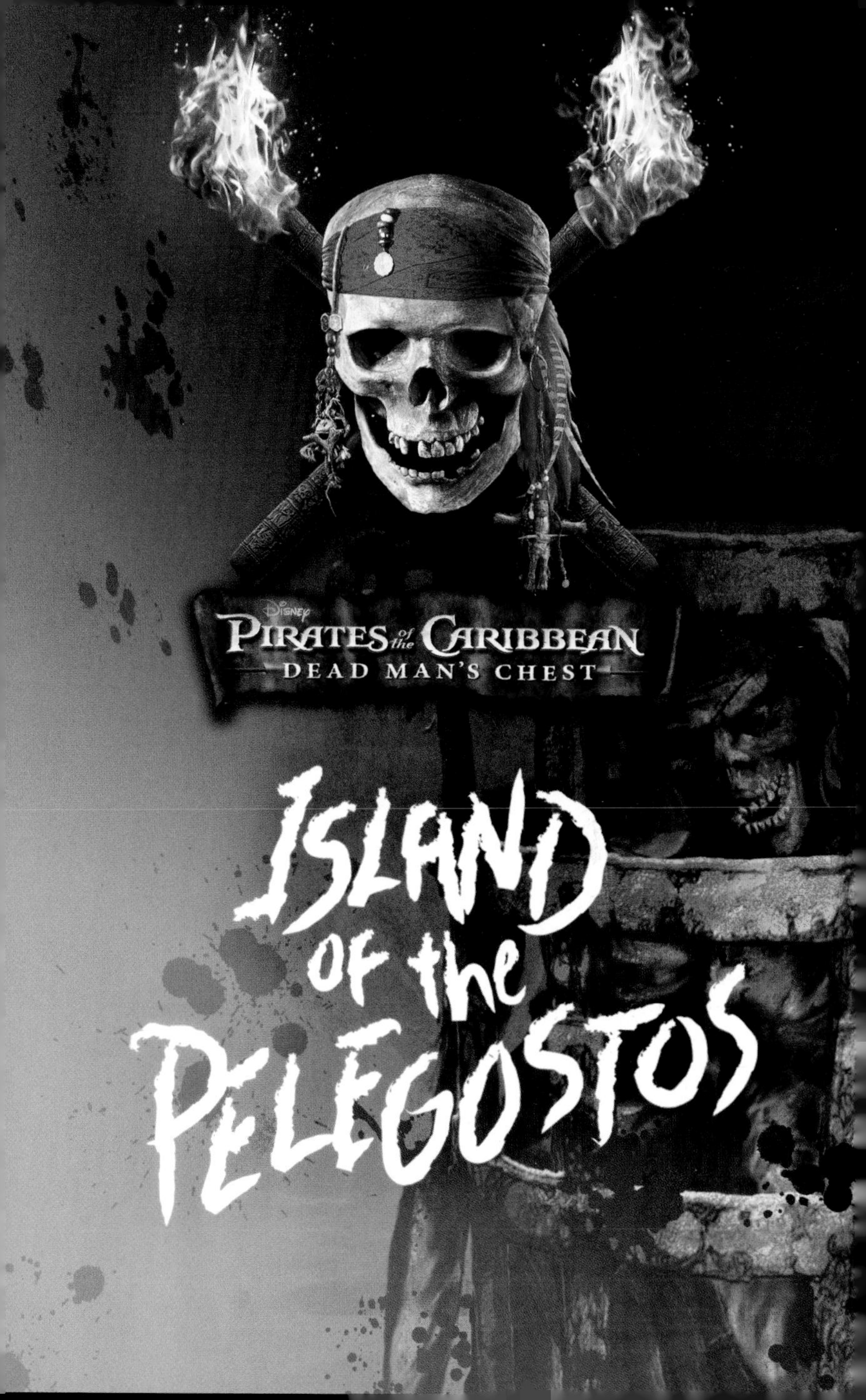
Disney
PIRATES of the CARIBBEAN
DEAD MAN'S CHEST
ISLAND of the PELEGOSTOS

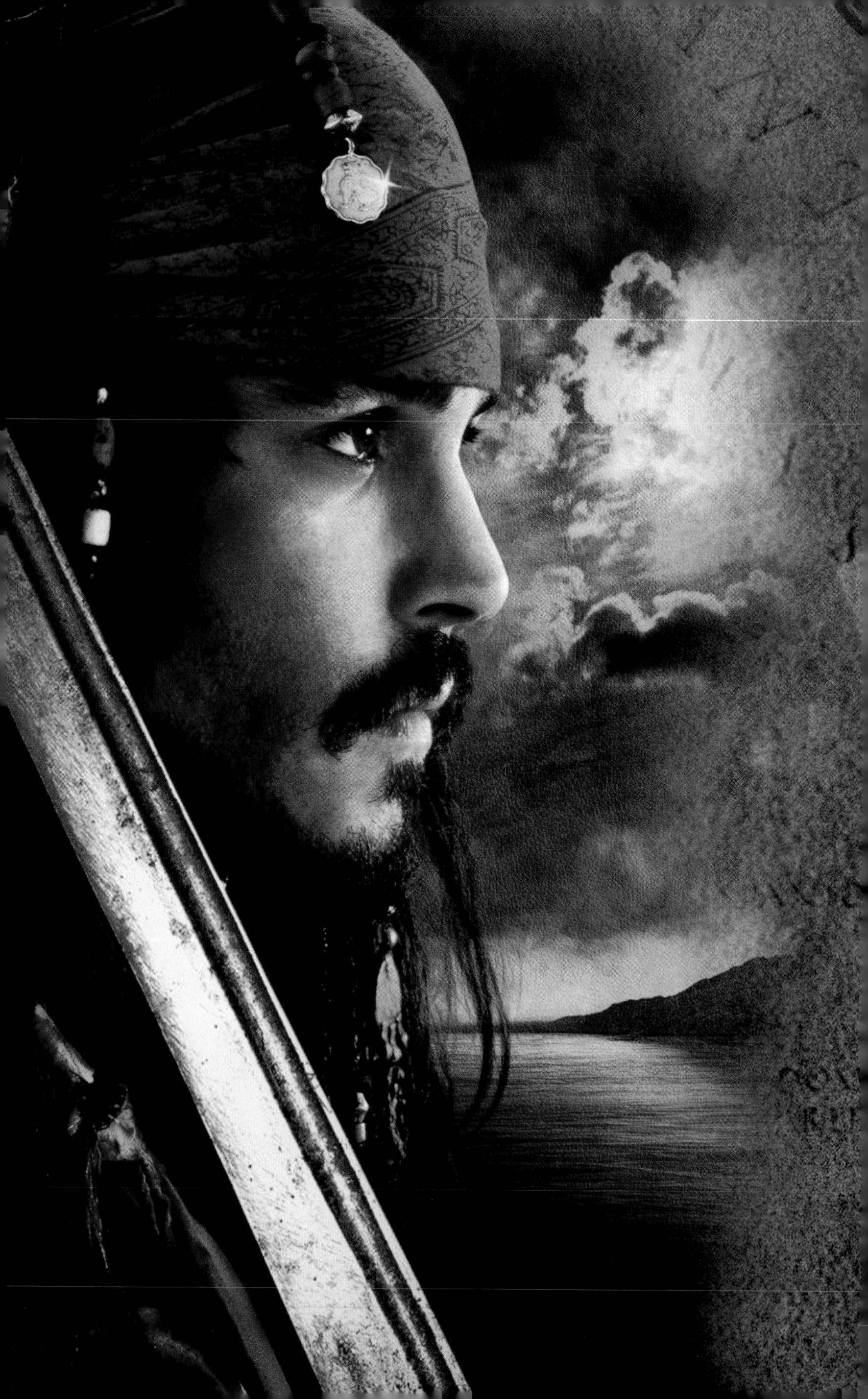

Portrait Gallery

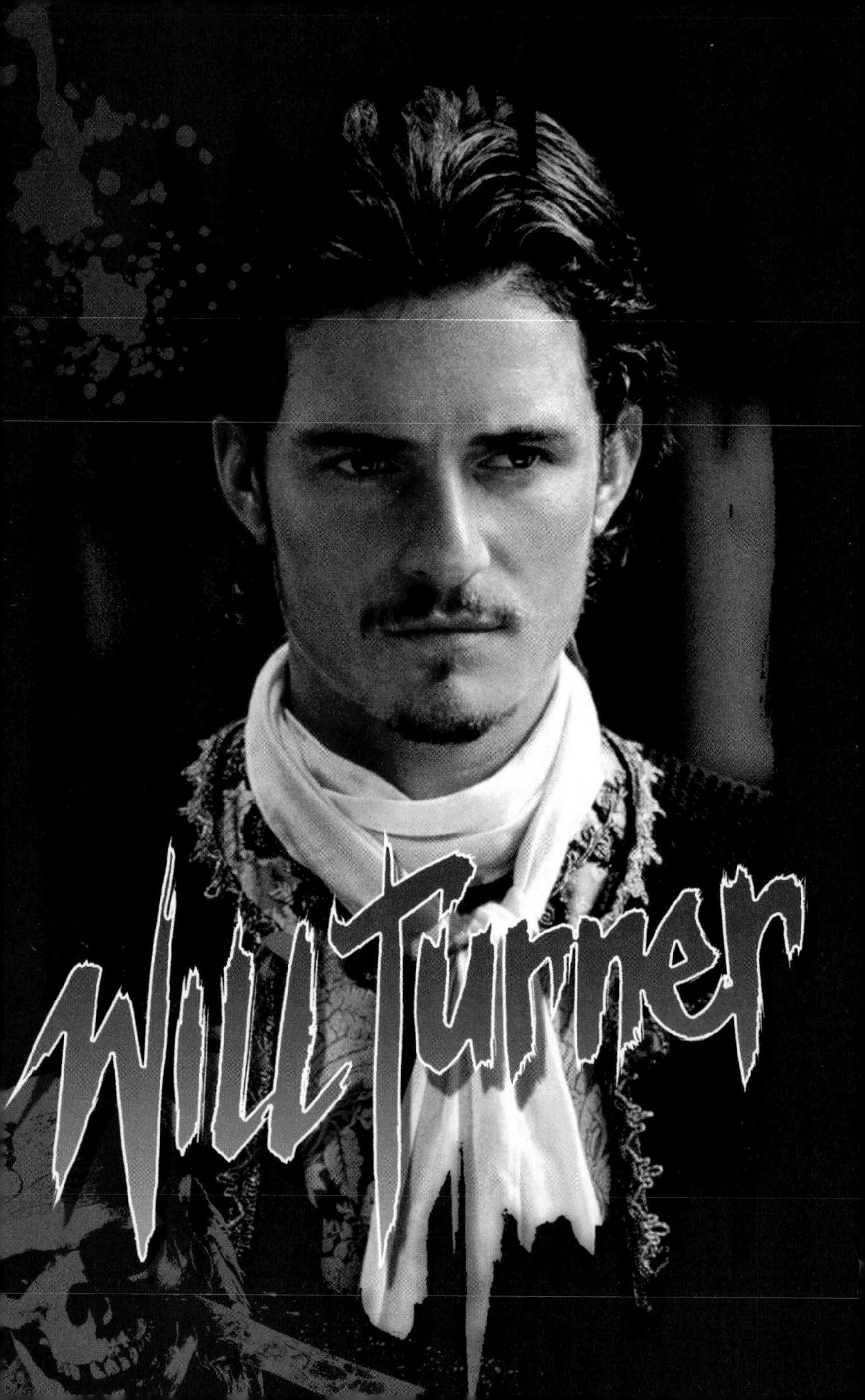
Will Turner

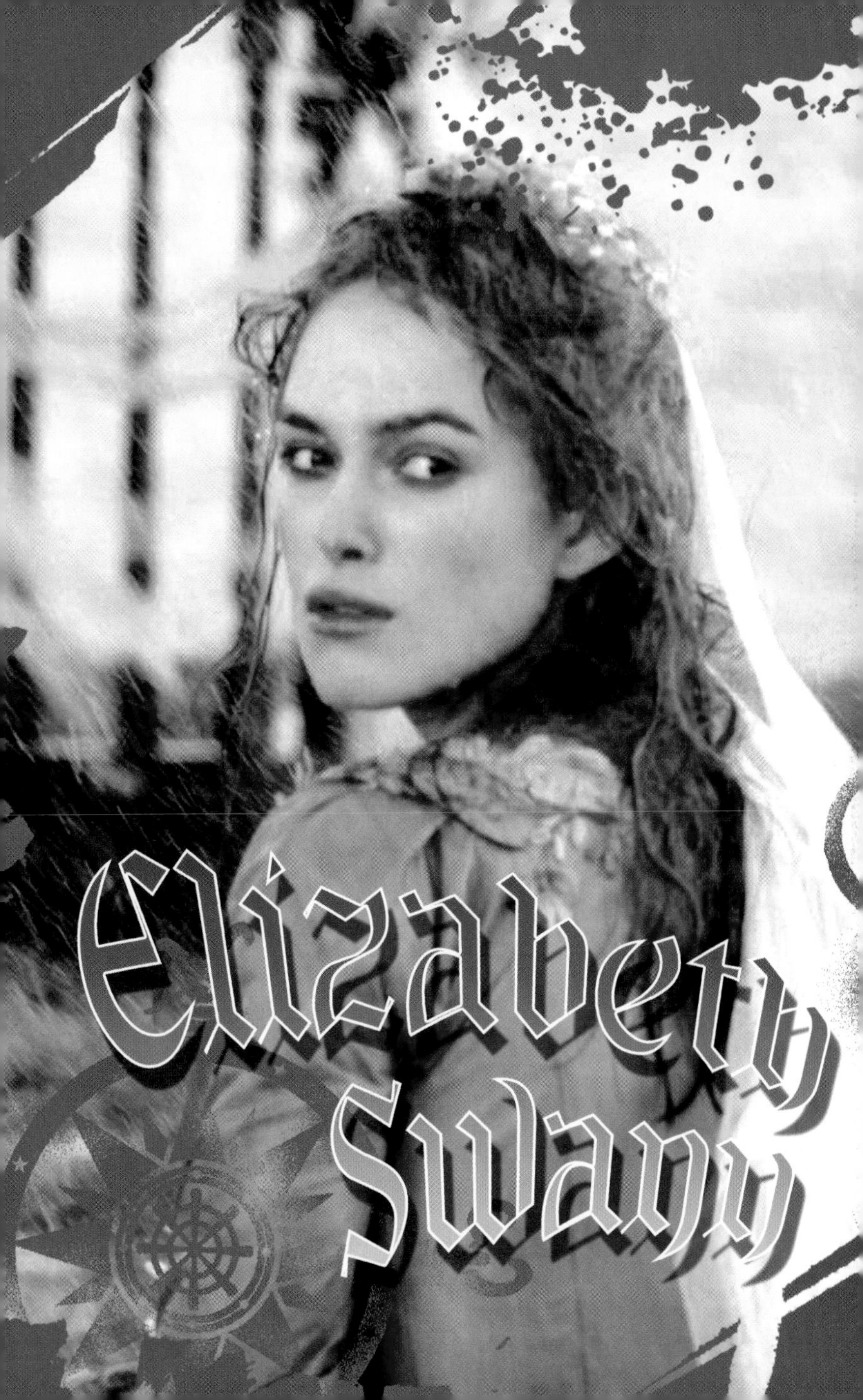
Elizabeth
Swann

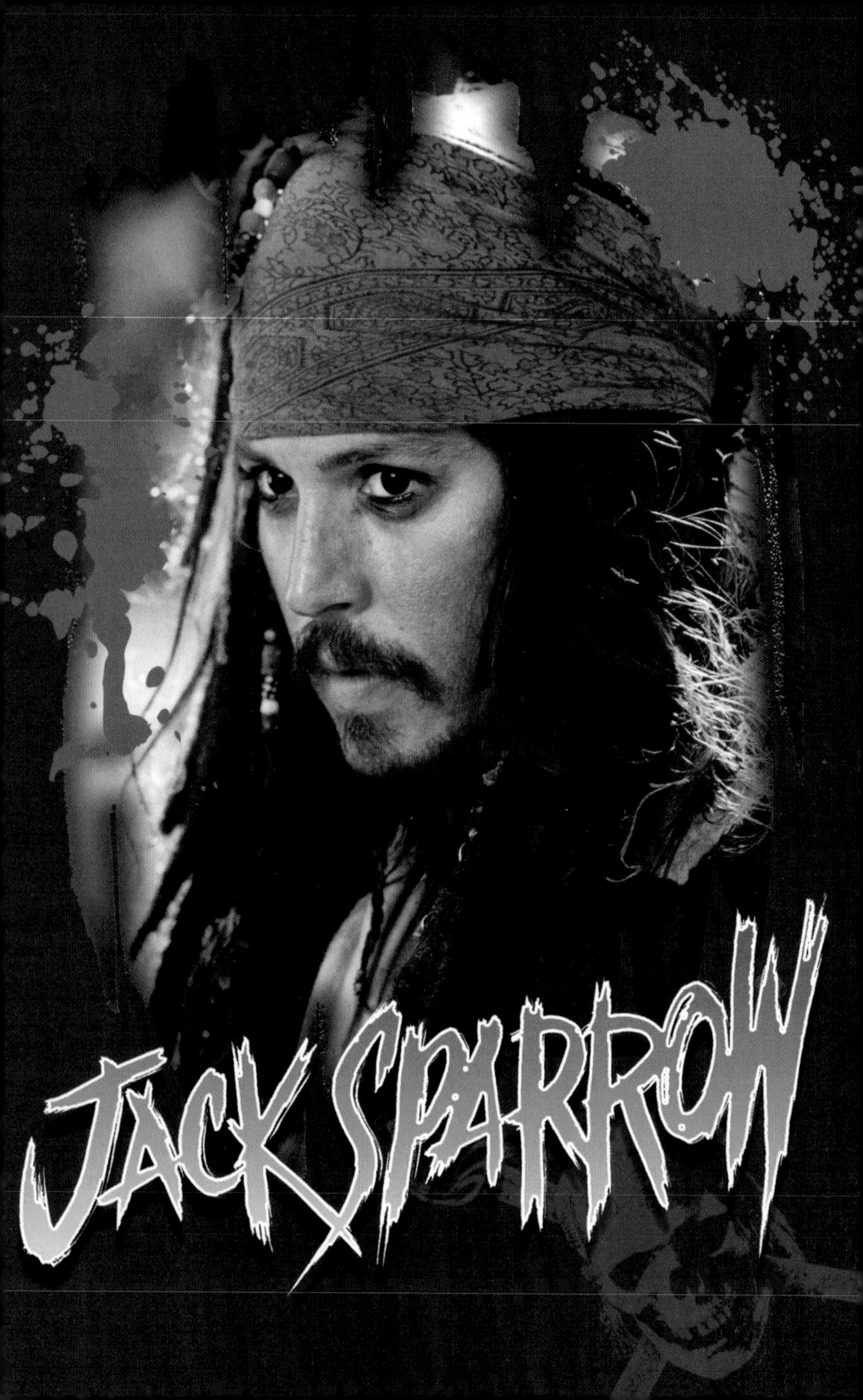
JACK SPARROW

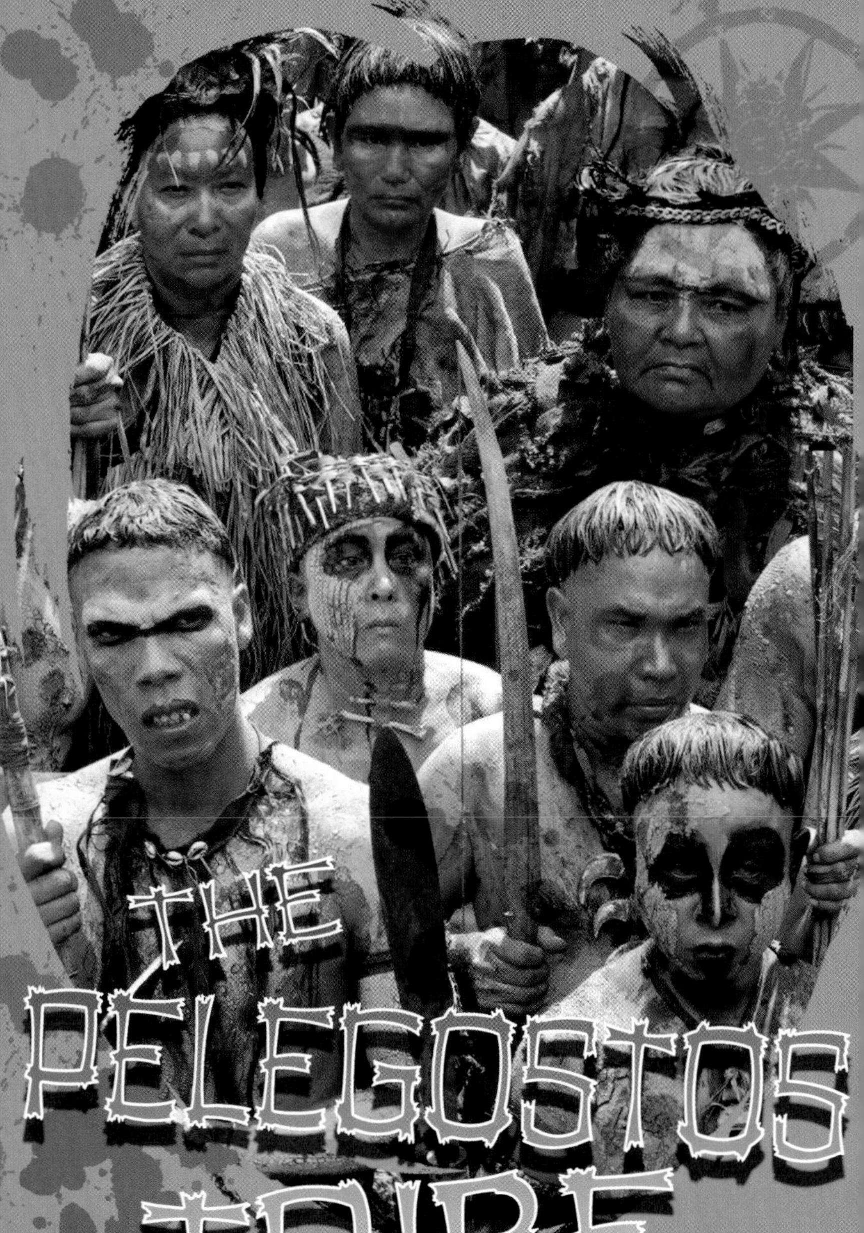

THE PELEGOSTOS TRIBE

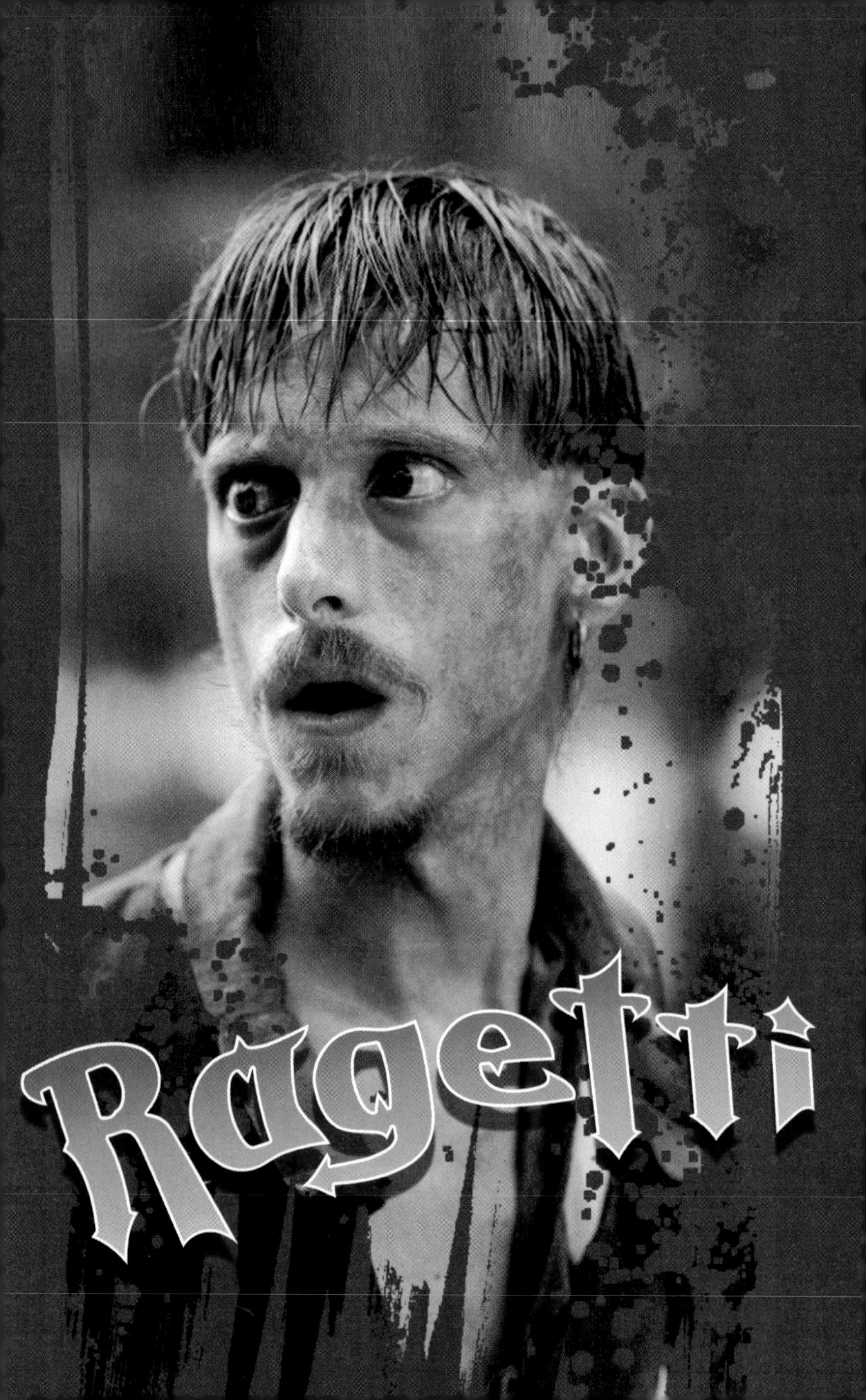
Ragetti

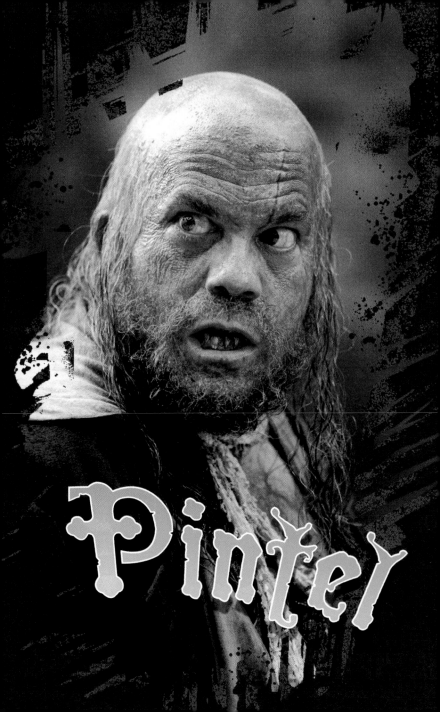

Pintel

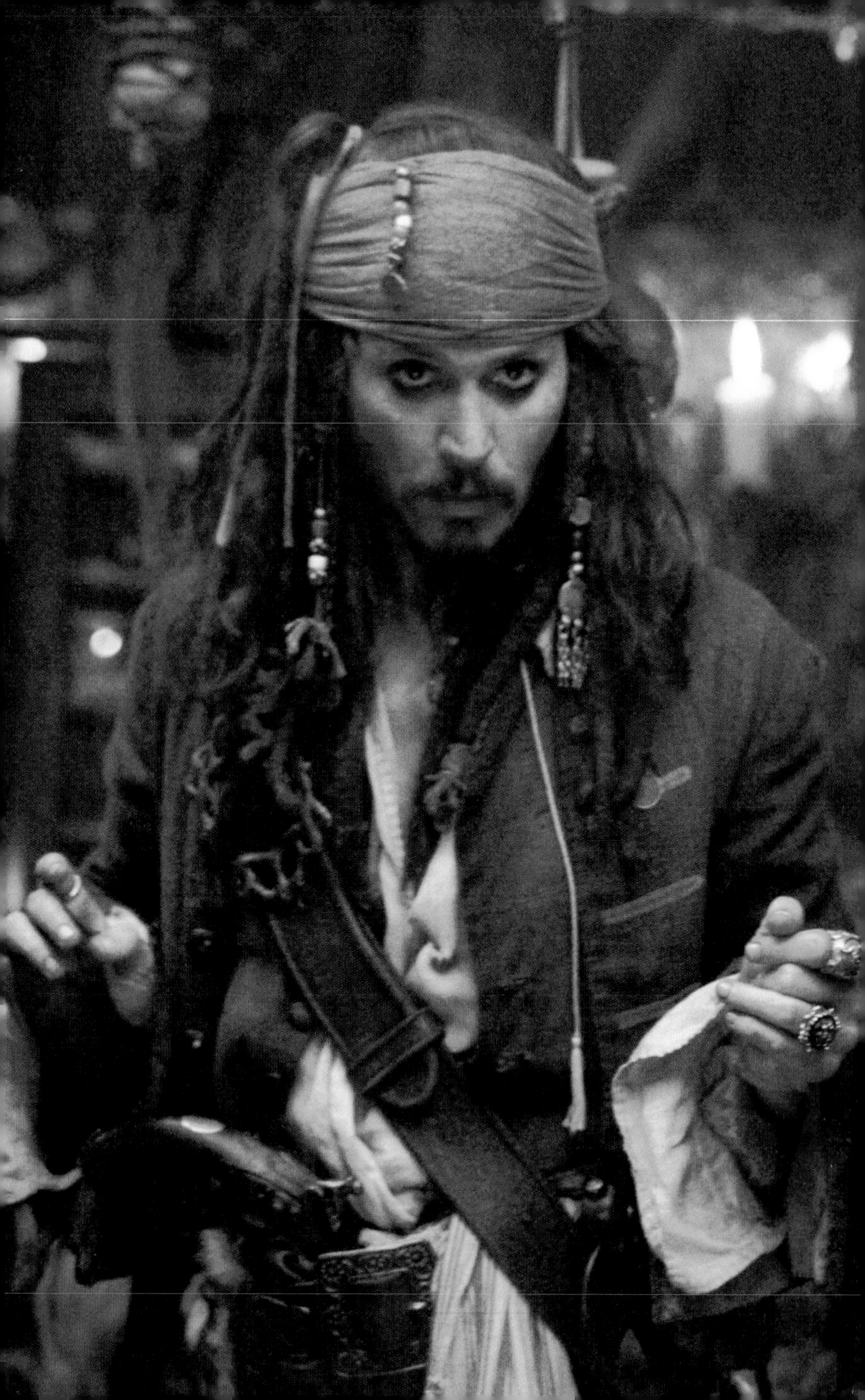

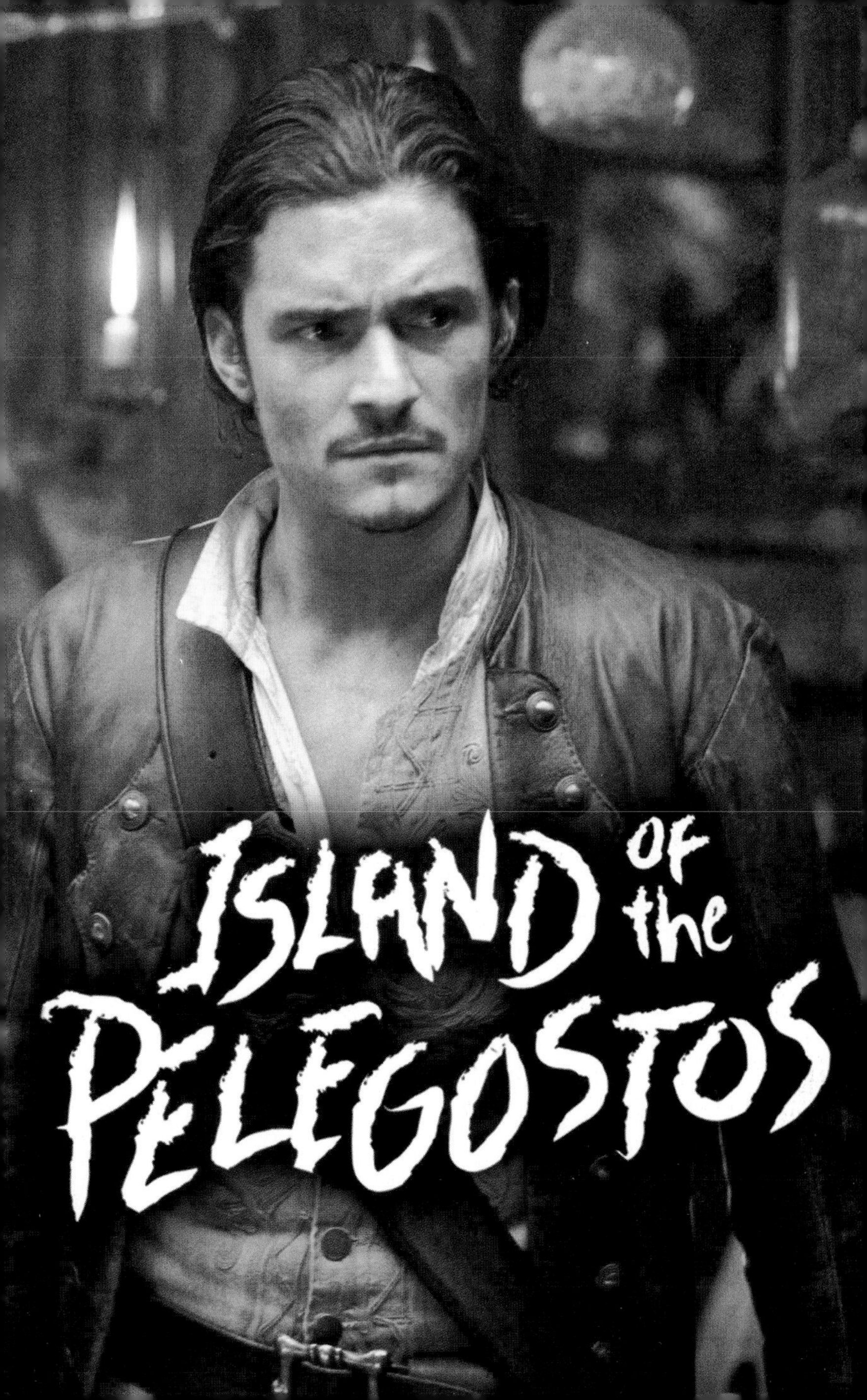
ISLAND of the
PELEGOSTOS

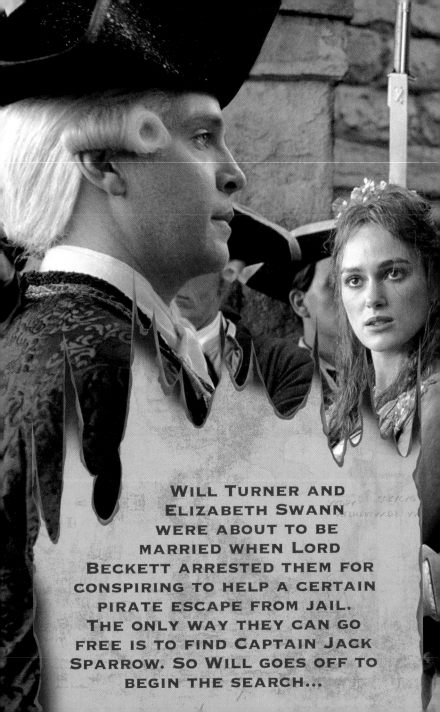

WILL TURNER AND
ELIZABETH SWANN
WERE ABOUT TO BE
MARRIED WHEN LORD
BECKETT ARRESTED THEM FOR
CONSPIRING TO HELP A CERTAIN
PIRATE ESCAPE FROM JAIL.
THE ONLY WAY THEY CAN GO
FREE IS TO FIND CAPTAIN JACK
SPARROW. SO WILL GOES OFF TO
BEGIN THE SEARCH...

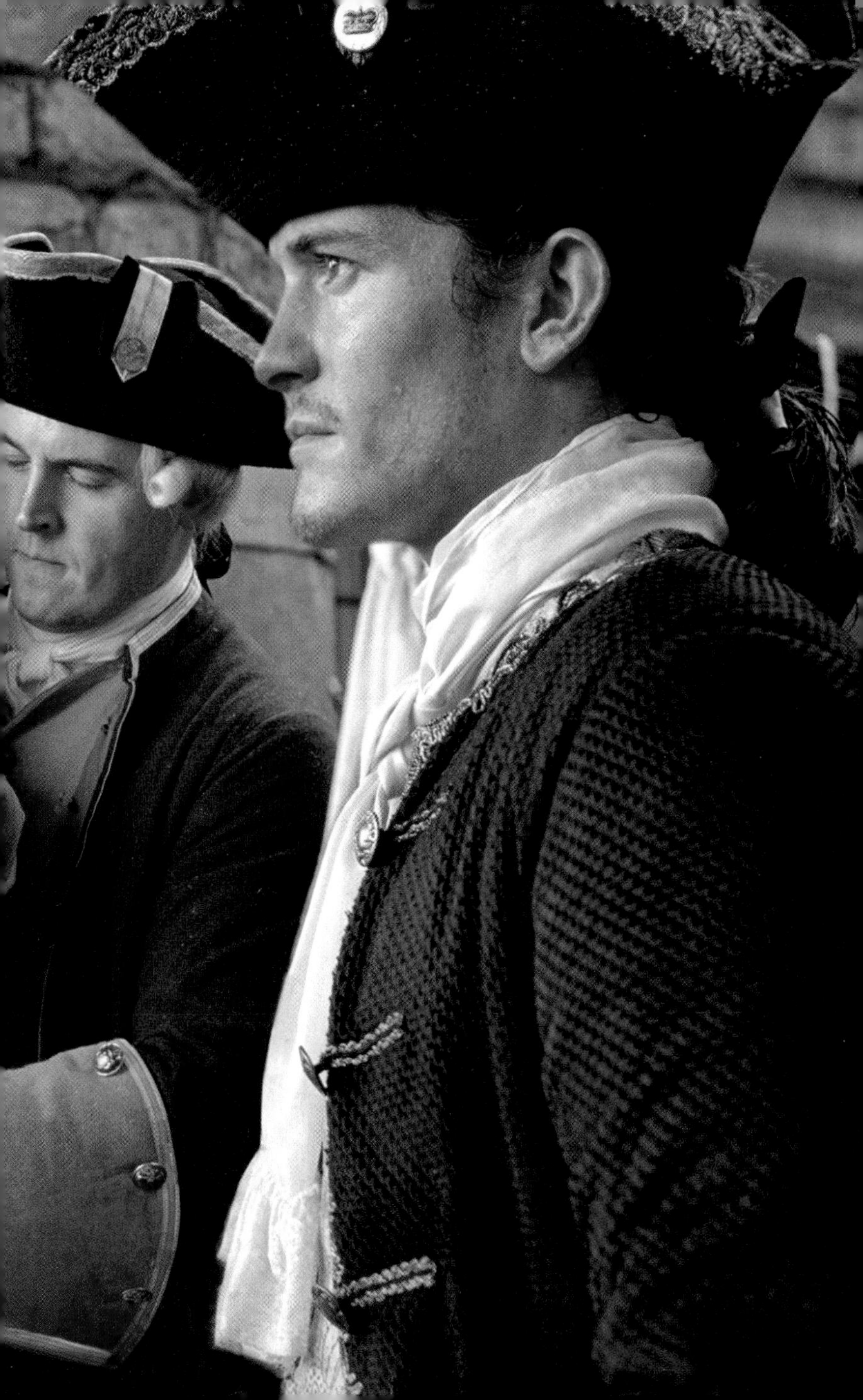

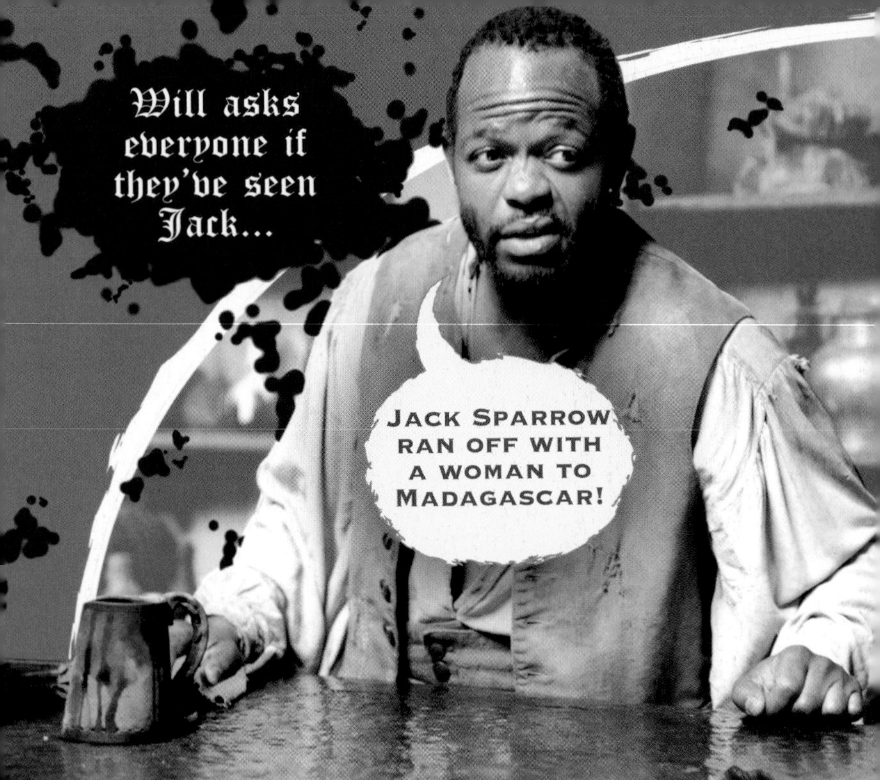
Will asks everyone if they've seen Jack...
JACK SPARROW RAN OFF WITH A WOMAN TO MADAGASCAR!

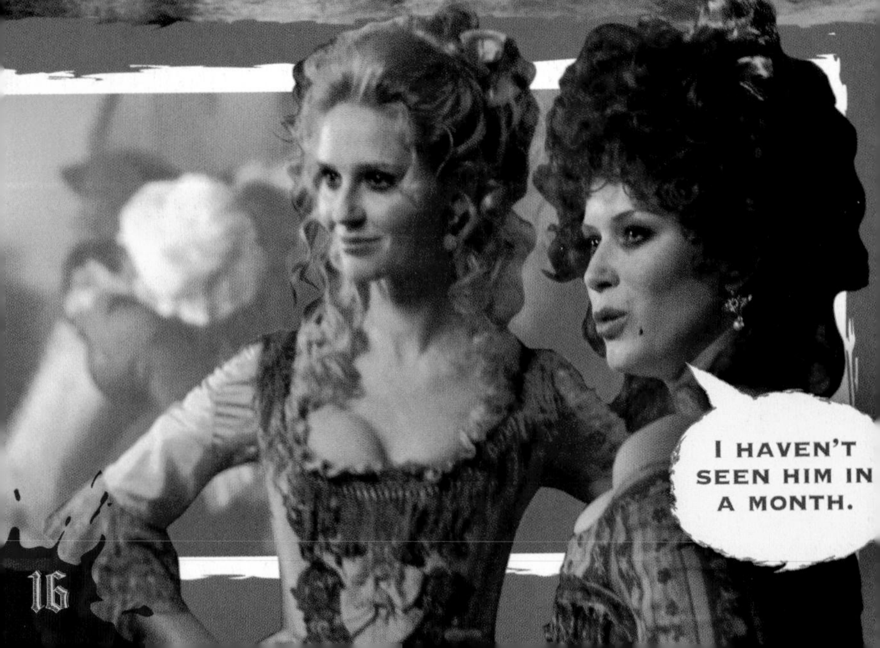
I HAVEN'T SEEN HIM IN A MONTH.

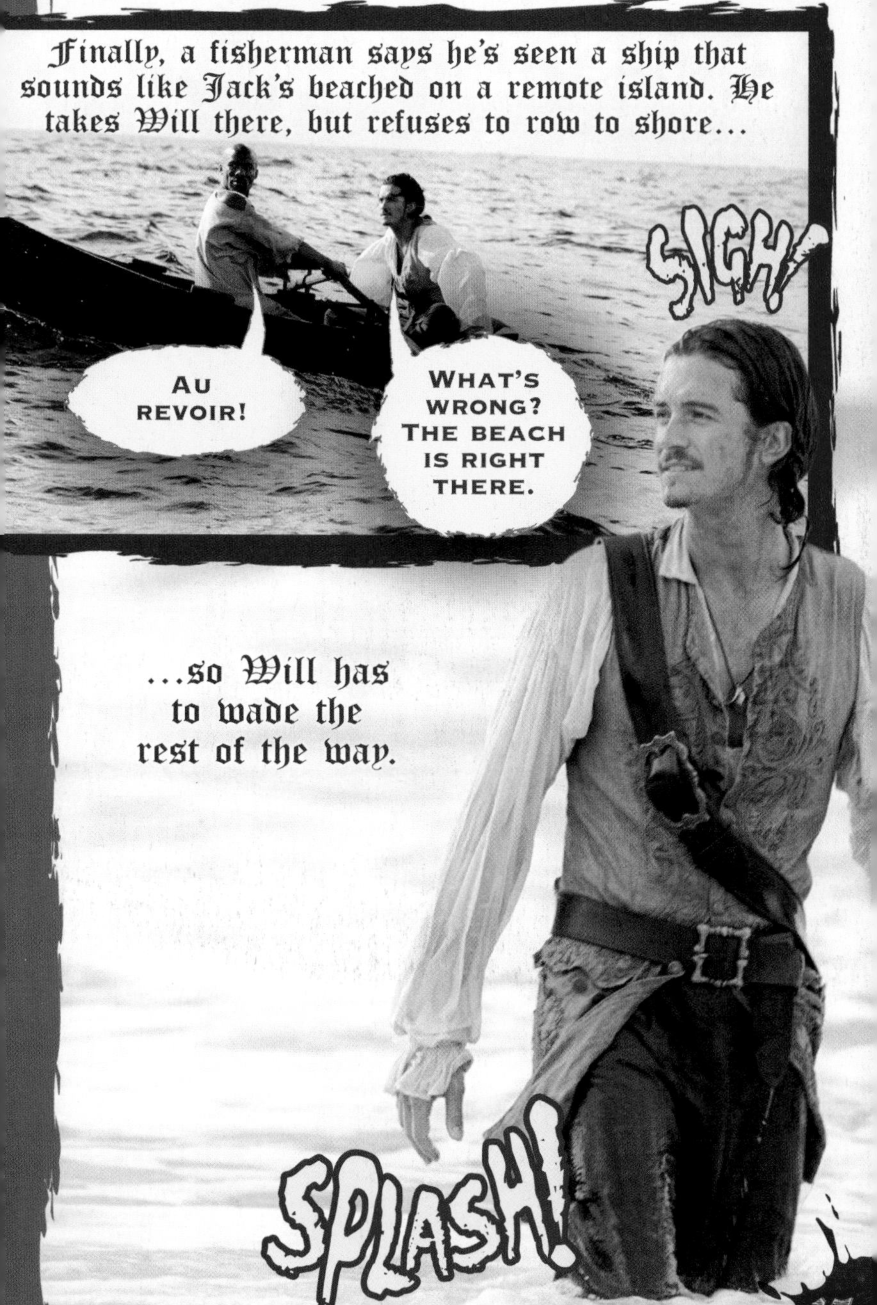
Finally, a fisherman says he's seen a ship that sounds like Jack's beached on a remote island. He takes Will there, but refuses to row to shore...
AU REVOIR!
WHAT'S WRONG? THE BEACH IS RIGHT THERE.
SIGH!
...so Will has to wade the rest of the way.
SPLASH!

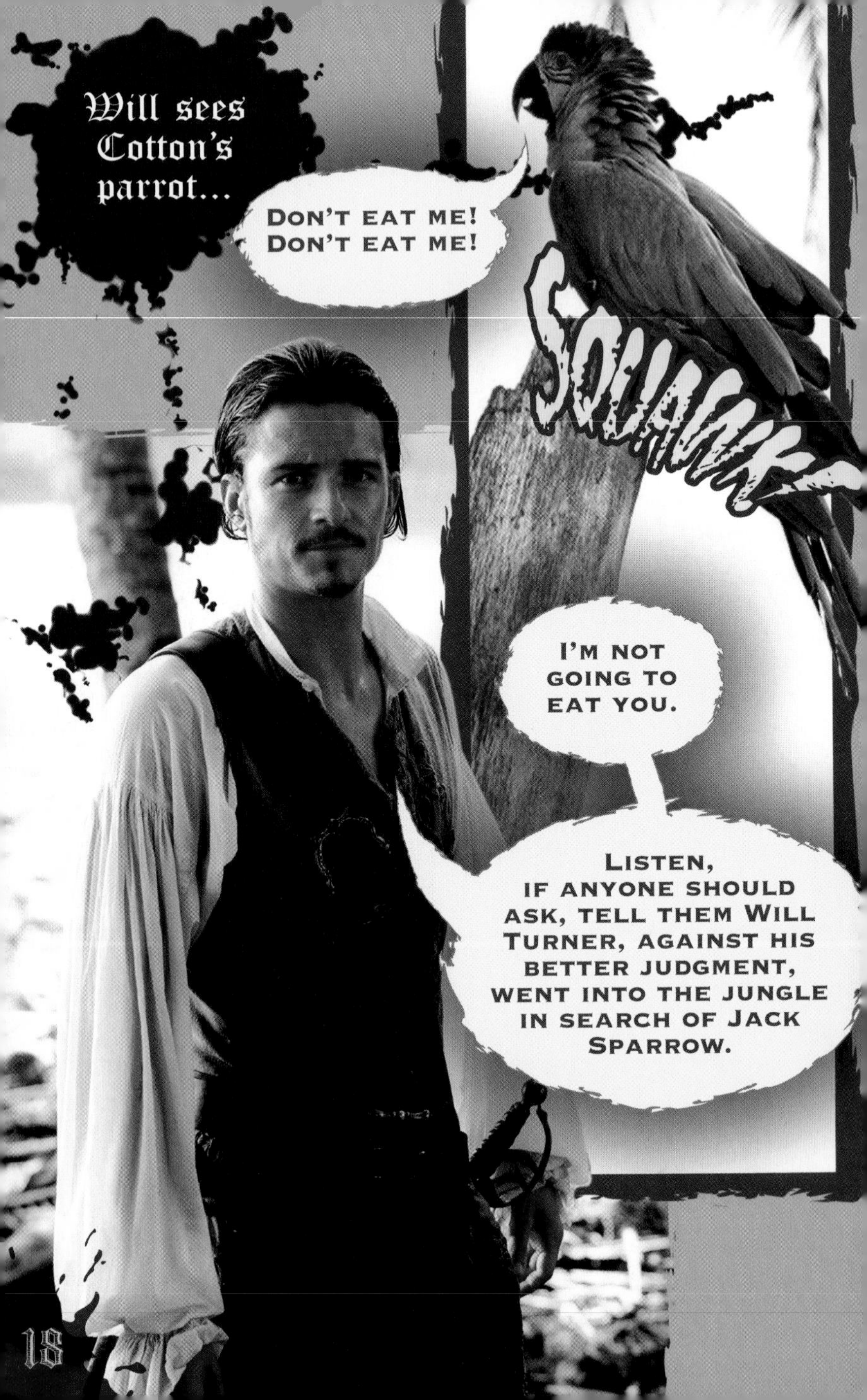
Will sees Cotton's parrot...
DON'T EAT ME! DON'T EAT ME!
SQUAWK!
I'M NOT GOING TO EAT YOU.
LISTEN, IF ANYONE SHOULD ASK, TELL THEM WILL TURNER, AGAINST HIS BETTER JUDGMENT, WENT INTO THE JUNGLE IN SEARCH OF JACK SPARROW.

But before long, the natives capture Will, carry him through a strange village...

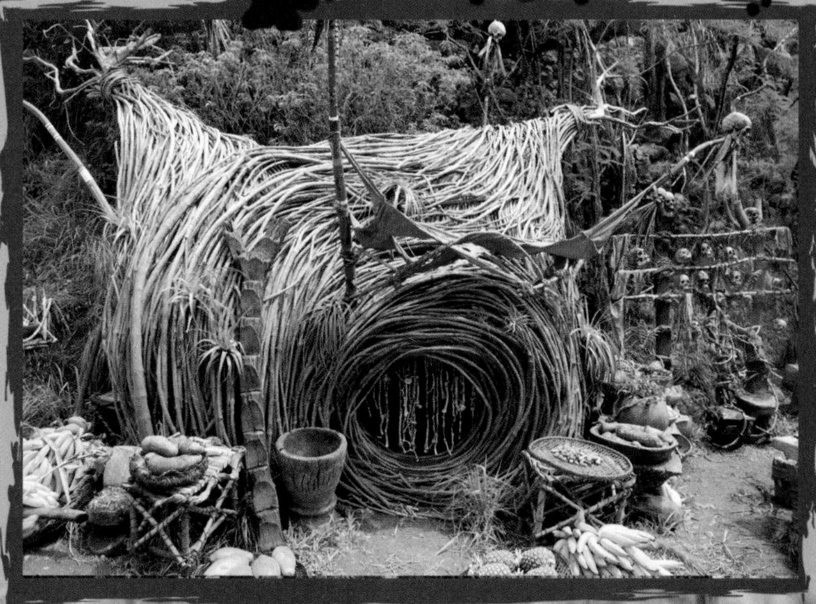

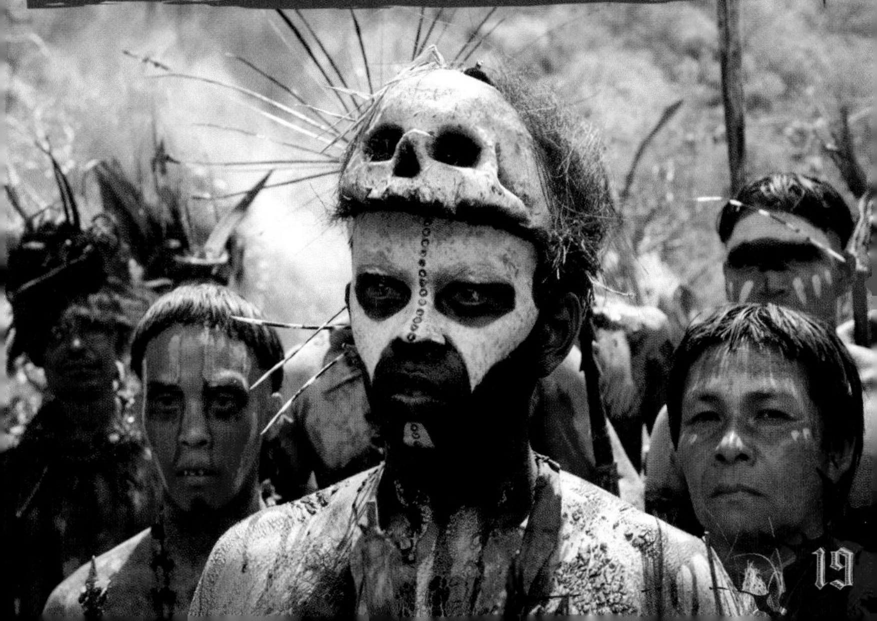

...and take him to their leader—
Captain Jack Sparrow!

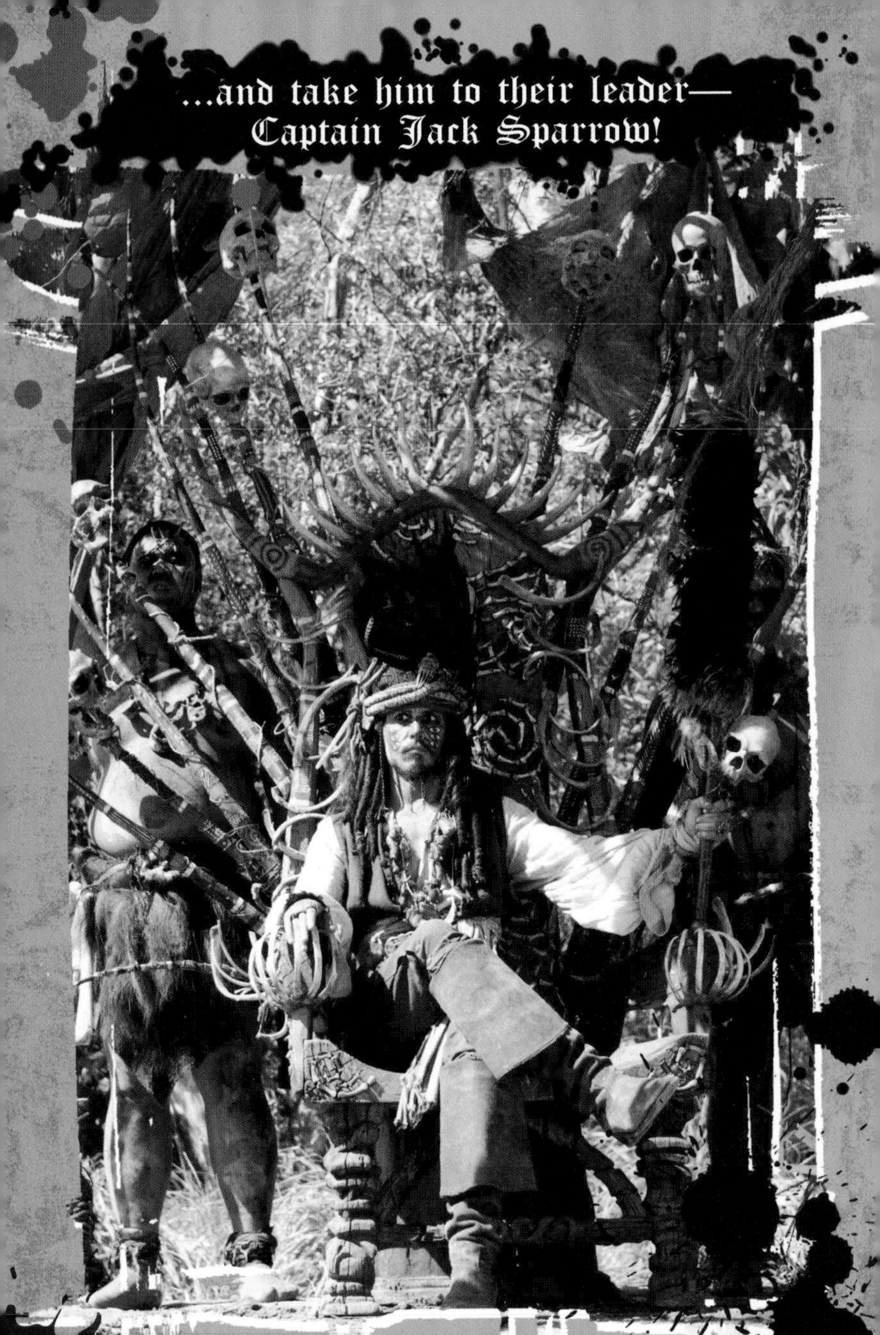

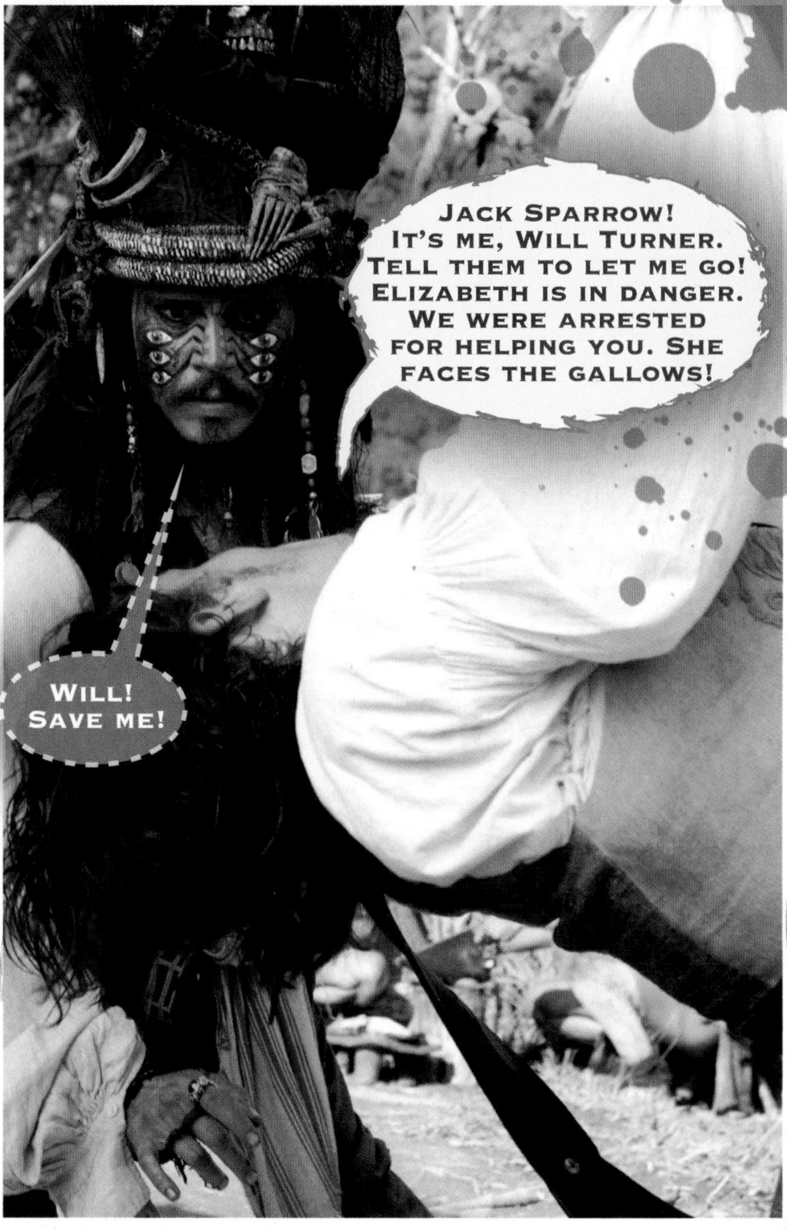
JACK SPARROW! IT'S ME, WILL TURNER. TELL THEM TO LET ME GO! ELIZABETH IS IN DANGER. WE WERE ARRESTED FOR HELPING YOU. SHE FACES THE GALLOWS!
WILL! SAVE ME!

The next thing he knows, Will is being thrown into a cage and hoisted up a tree with the rest of the Black Pearl crew.

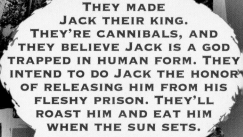

WHY WOULD JACK LOCK US UP IN HERE? IF HE'S THE KING--

THEY MADE JACK THEIR KING. THEY'RE CANNIBALS, AND THEY BELIEVE JACK IS A GOD TRAPPED IN HUMAN FORM. THEY INTEND TO DO JACK THE HONOR OF RELEASING HIM FROM HIS FLESHY PRISON. THEY'LL ROAST HIM AND EAT HIM WHEN THE SUN SETS.

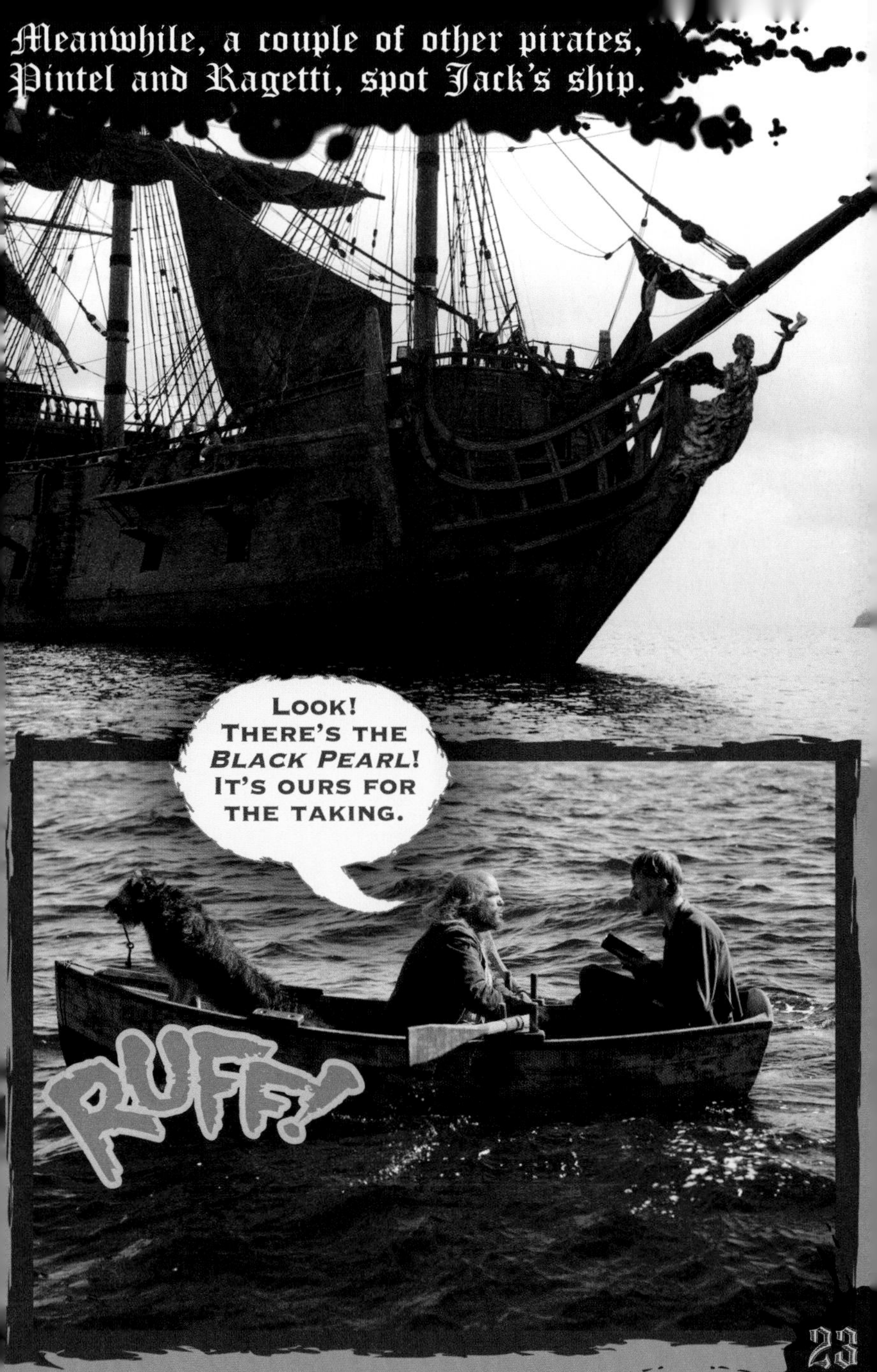
Meanwhile, a couple of other pirates, Pintel and Ragetti, spot Jack's ship.
LOOK! THERE'S THE *BLACK PEARL*! IT'S OURS FOR THE TAKING.
RUFF!

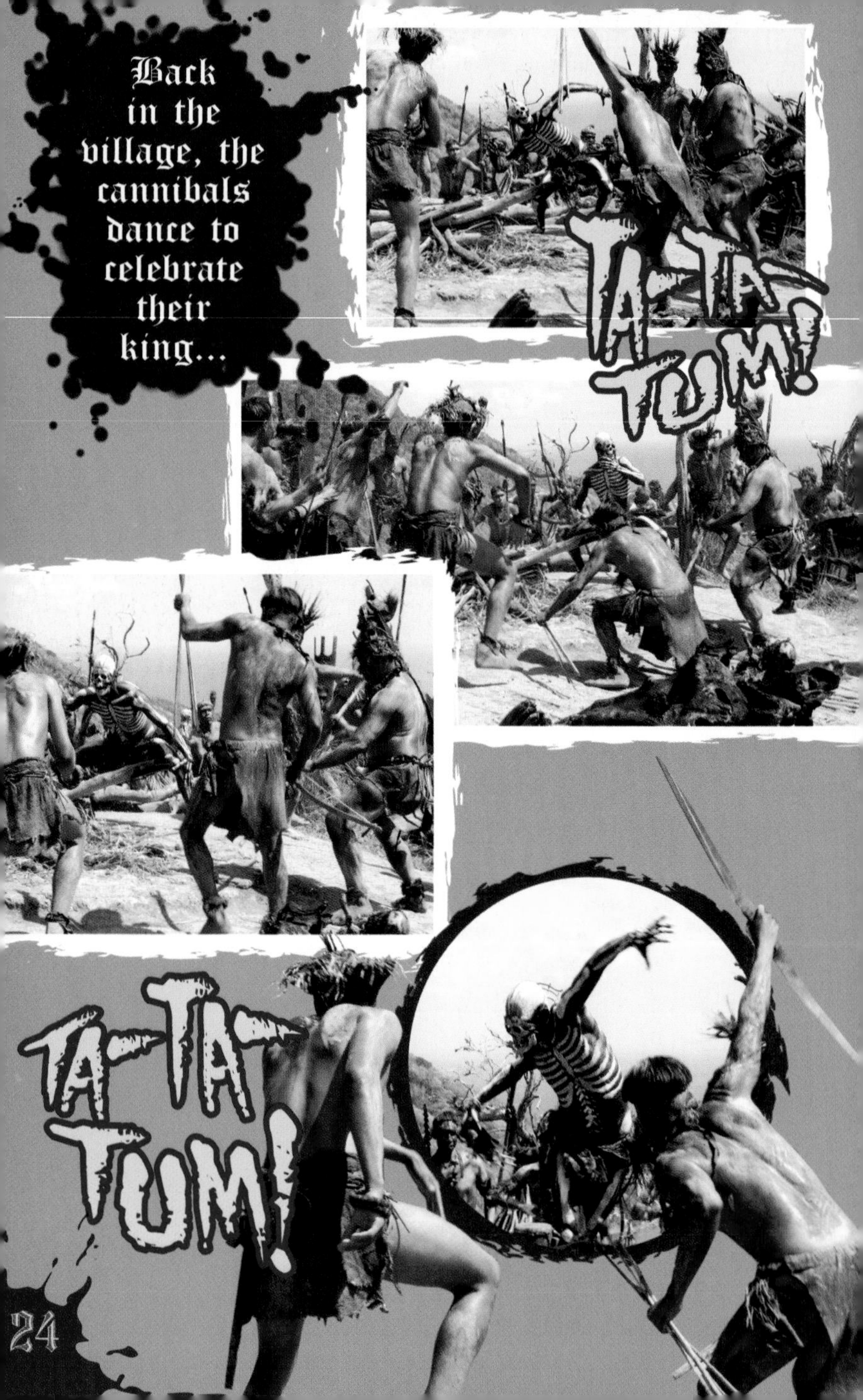
Back in the village, the cannibals dance to celebrate their king...
TA-TA TUM!
TA-TA TUM!

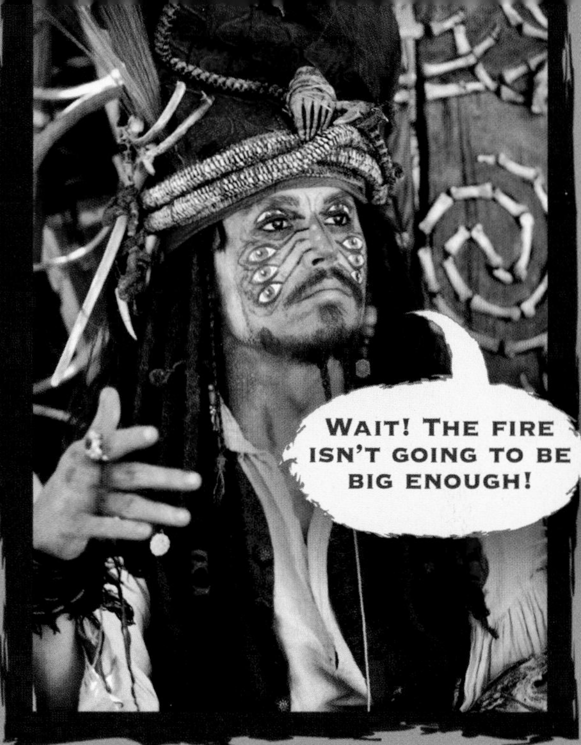
WAIT! THE FIRE ISN'T GOING TO BE BIG ENOUGH!

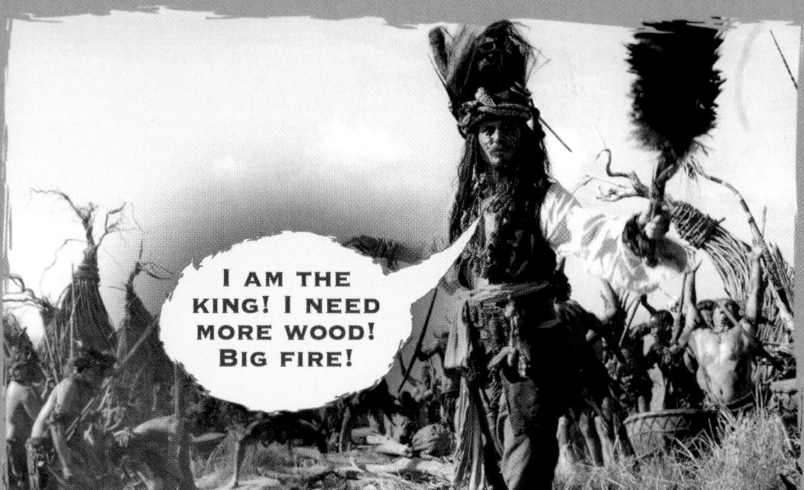
I AM THE KING! I NEED MORE WOOD! BIG FIRE!

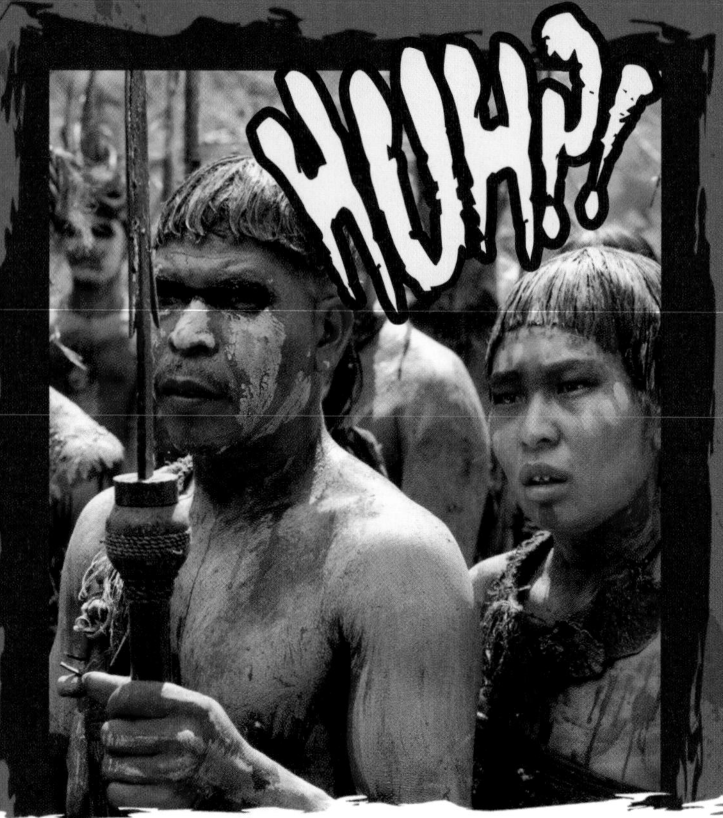
HUH?!

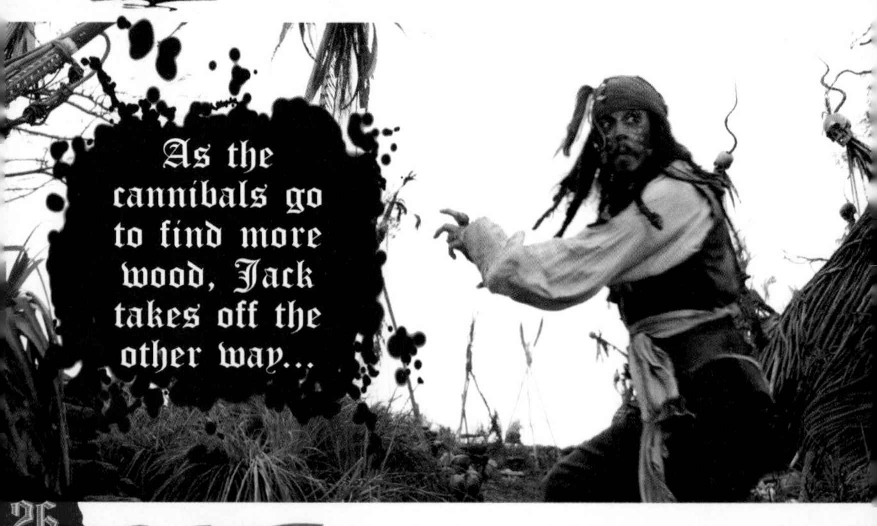
As the cannibals go to find more wood, Jack takes off the other way...

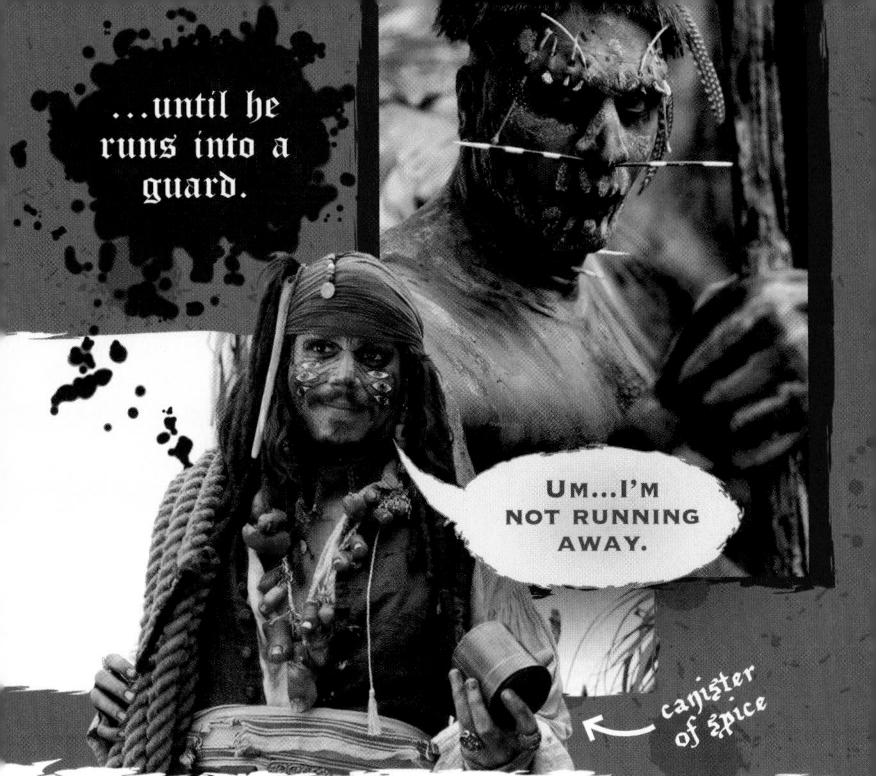
...until he runs into a guard.
UM...I'M NOT RUNNING AWAY.
canister of spice

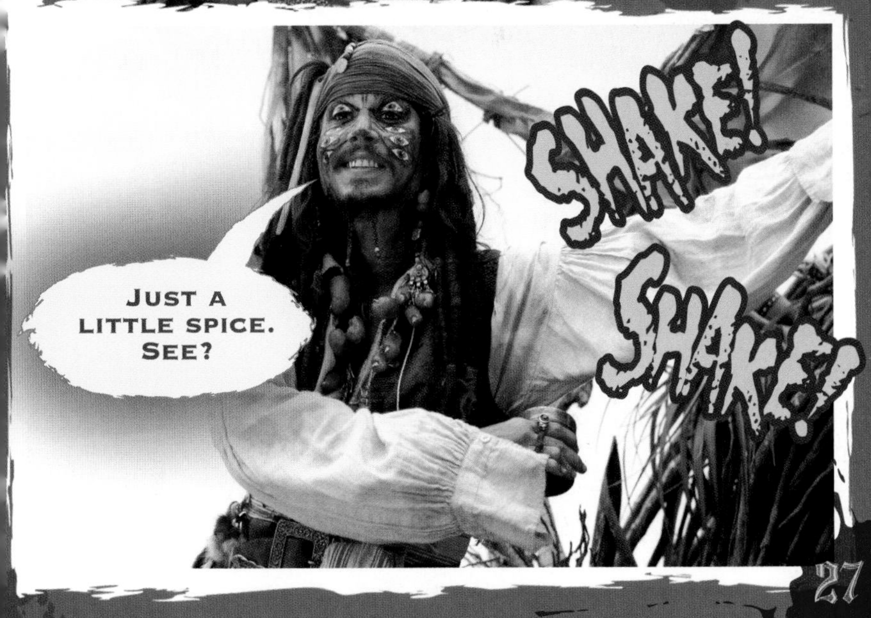
JUST A LITTLE SPICE. SEE?
SHAKE!
SHAKE!

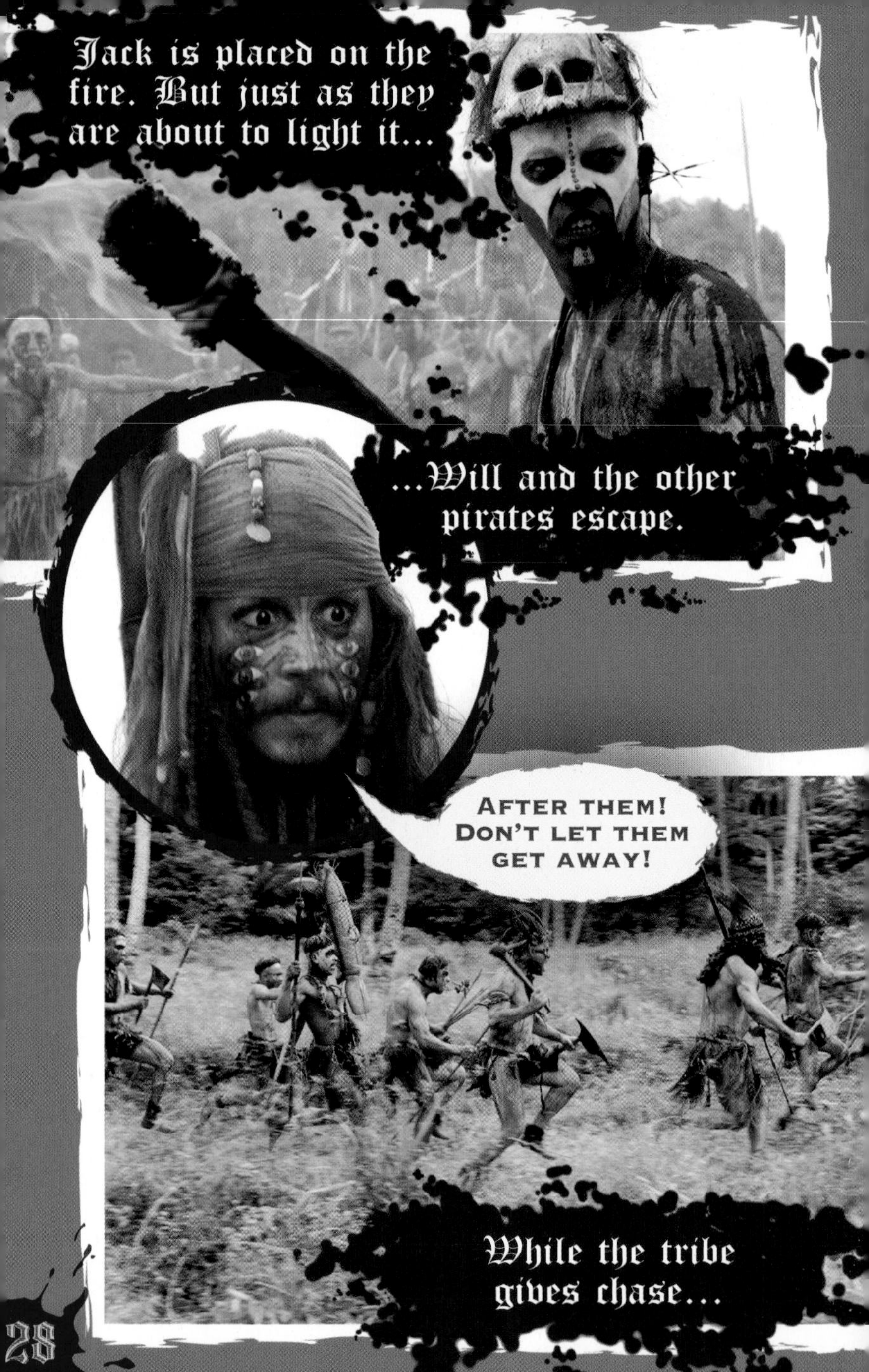
Jack is placed on the fire. But just as they are about to light it...
...Will and the other pirates escape.
AFTER THEM! DON'T LET THEM GET AWAY!
While the tribe gives chase...

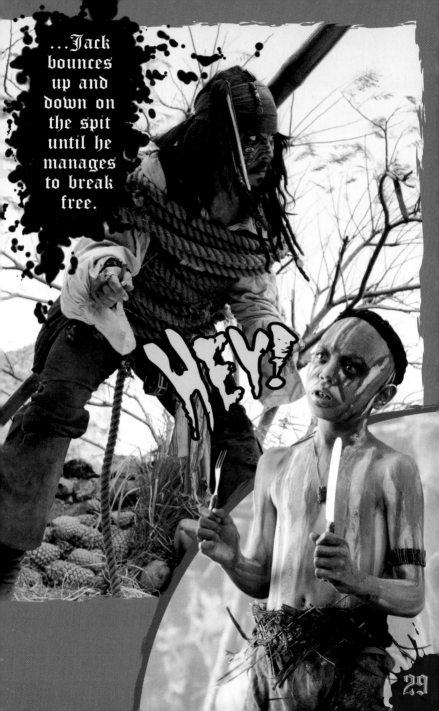

...Jack bounces up and down on the spit until he manages to break free.

HEY!

29

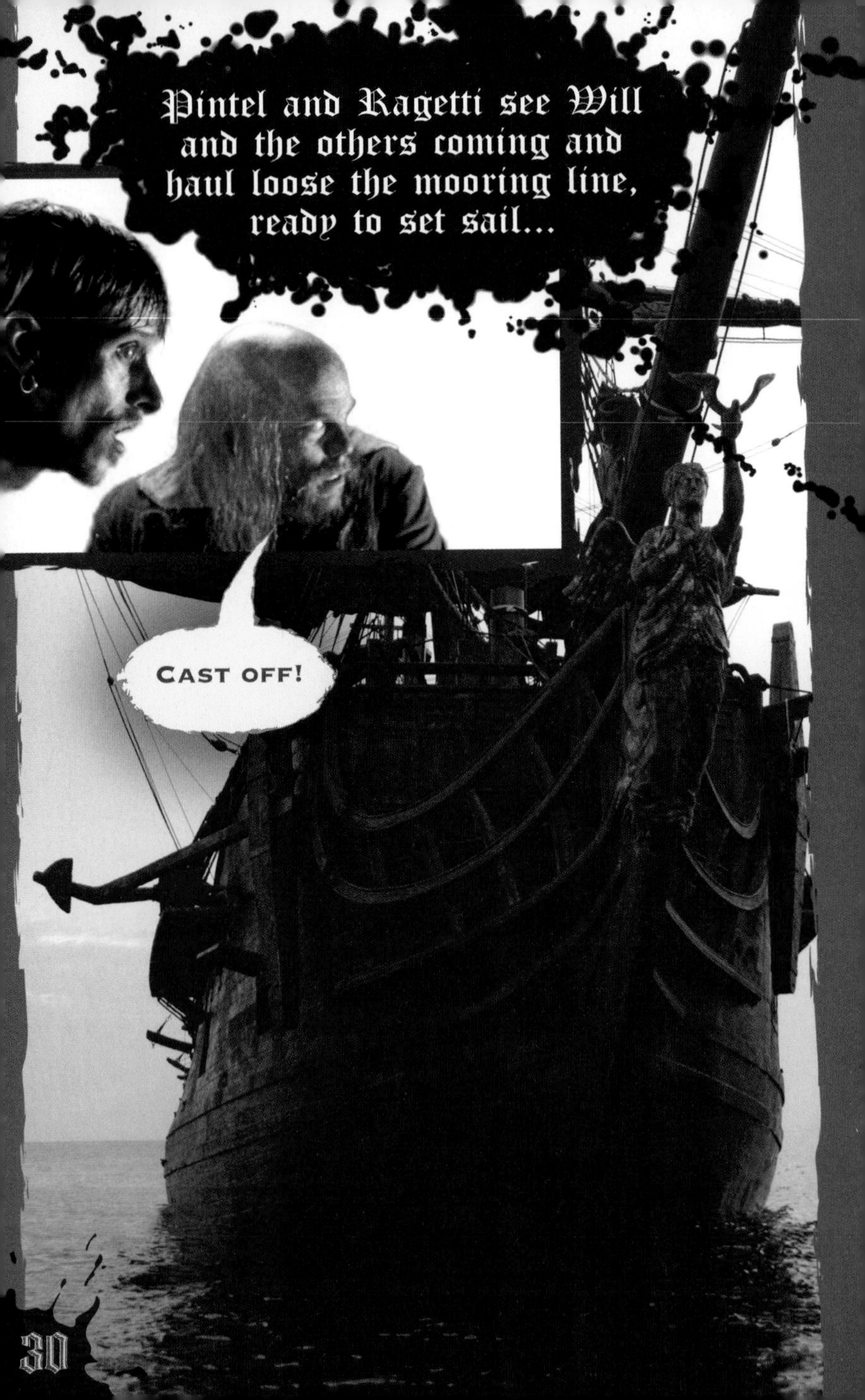
Pintel and Ragetti see Will and the others coming and haul loose the mooring line, ready to set sail...
CAST OFF!

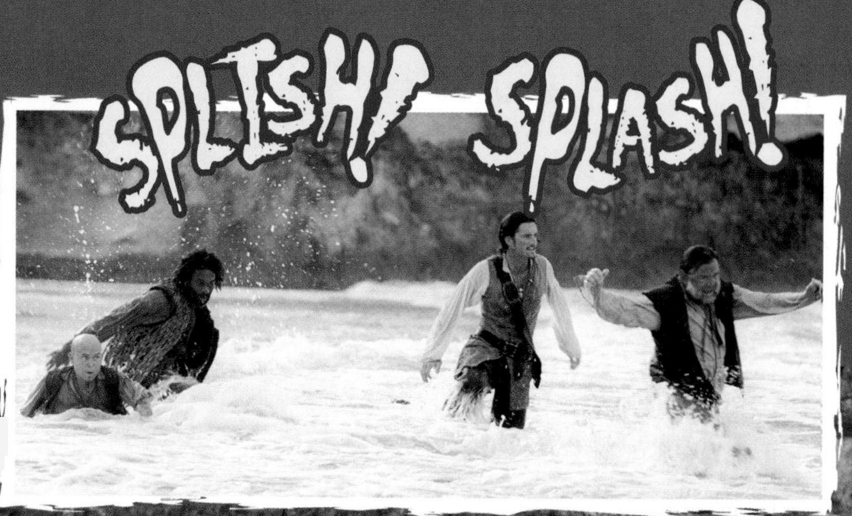
SPLISH! SPLASH!

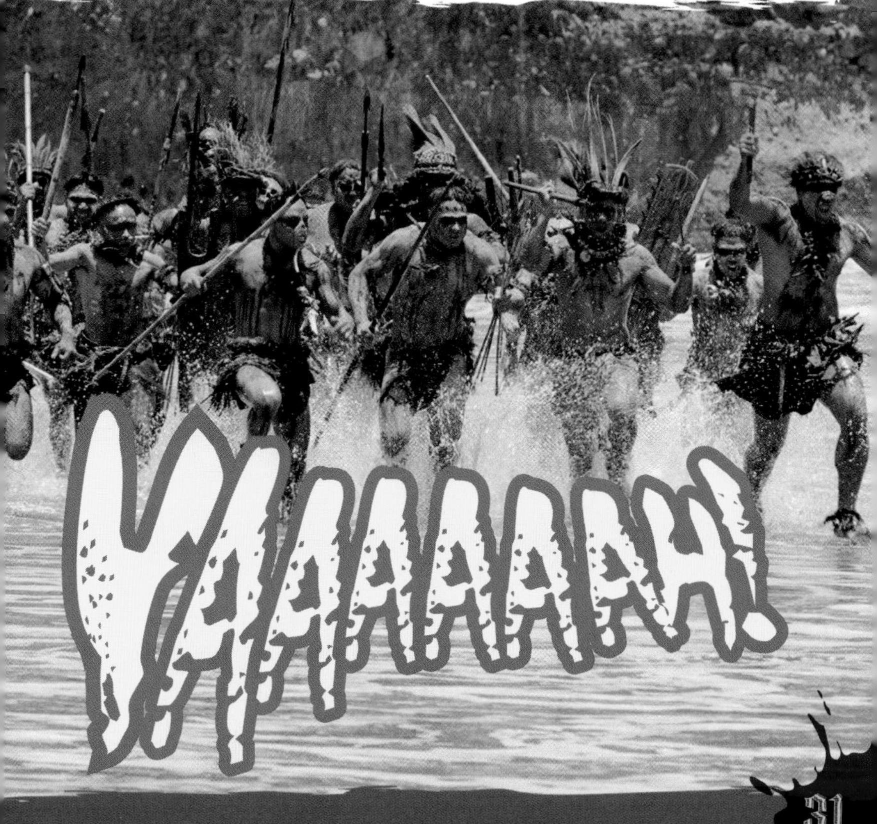
YAAAAAAH!

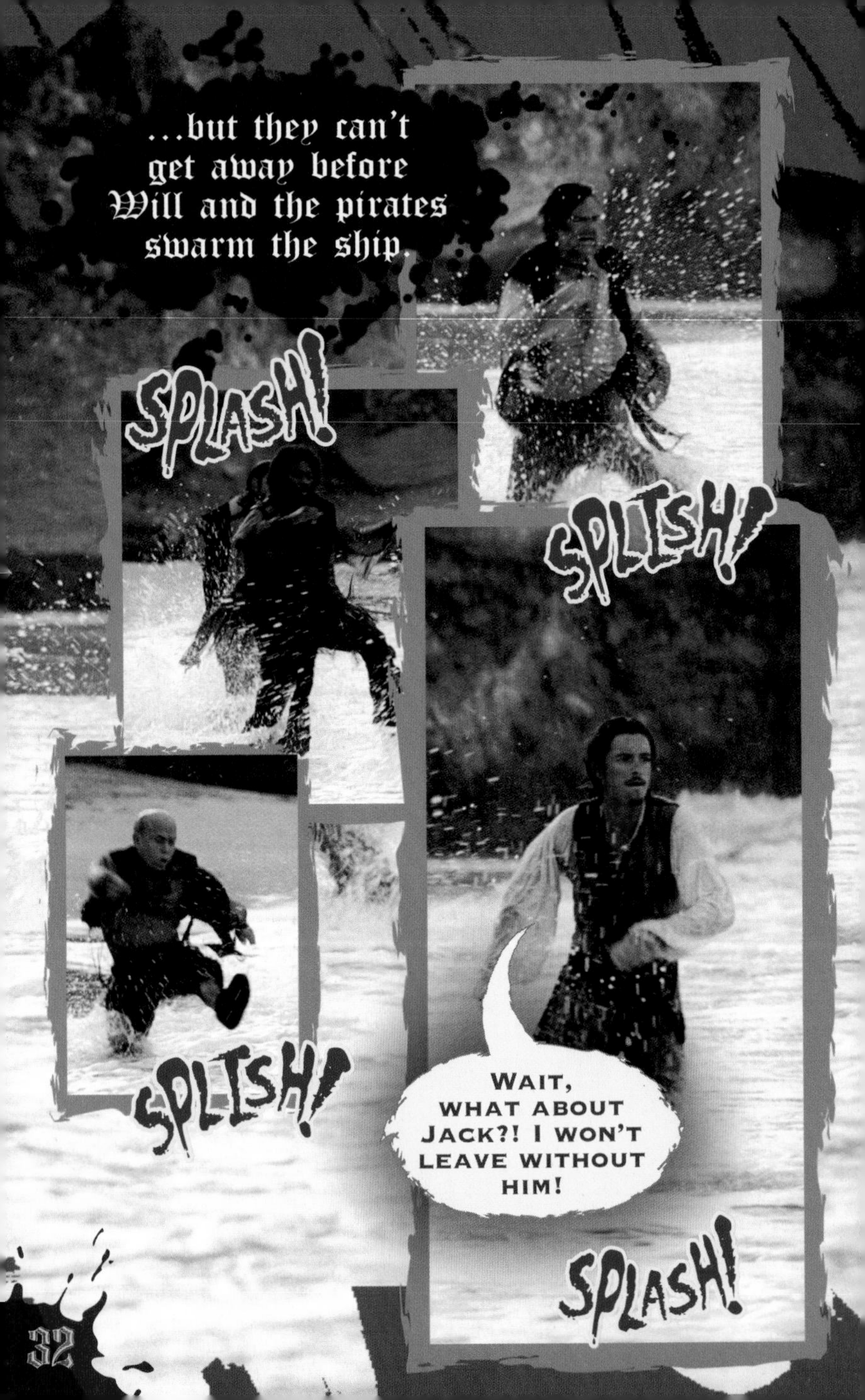
...but they can't get away before Will and the pirates swarm the ship.
SPLASH!
SPLISH!
SPLISH!
WAIT, WHAT ABOUT JACK?! I WON'T LEAVE WITHOUT HIM!
SPLASH!

Jack
is close
behind...

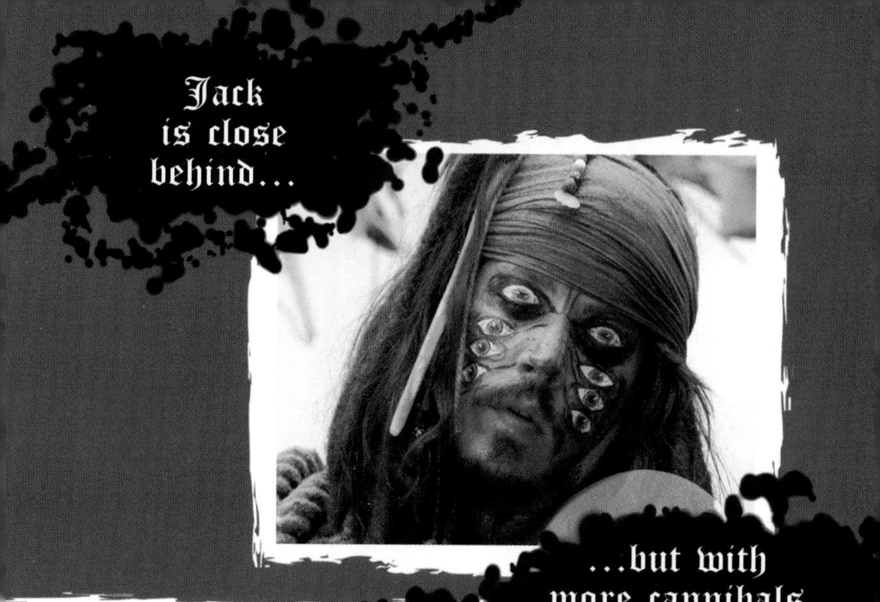

...but with
more cannibals
in hot pursuit!

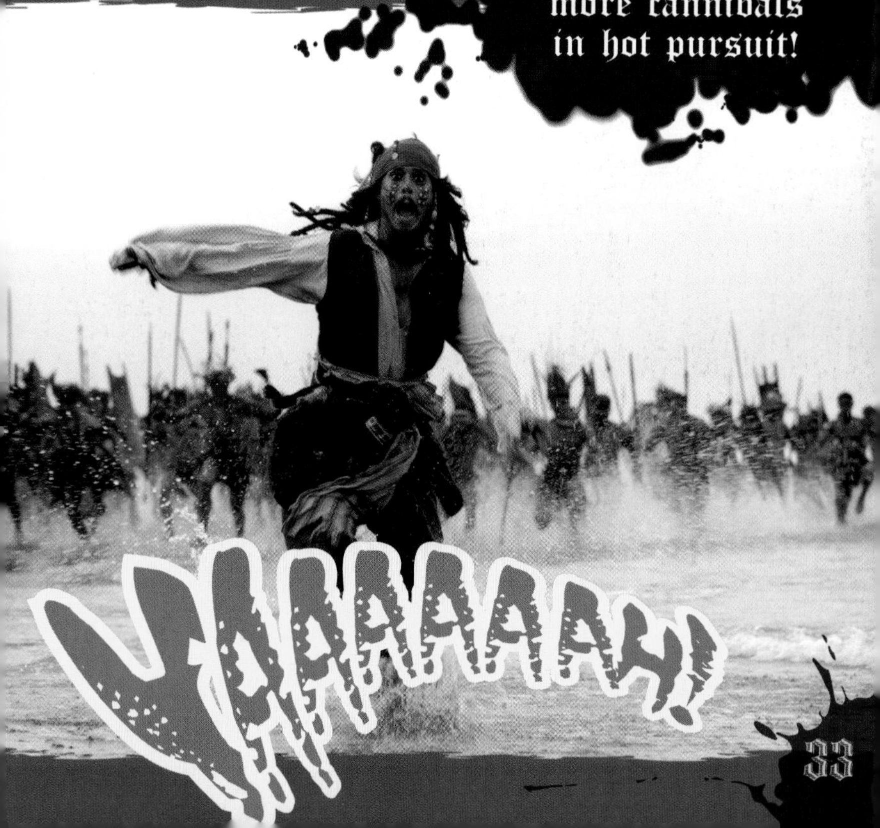
YAAAAAH!

Jack just manages to scramble aboard, and they're off!

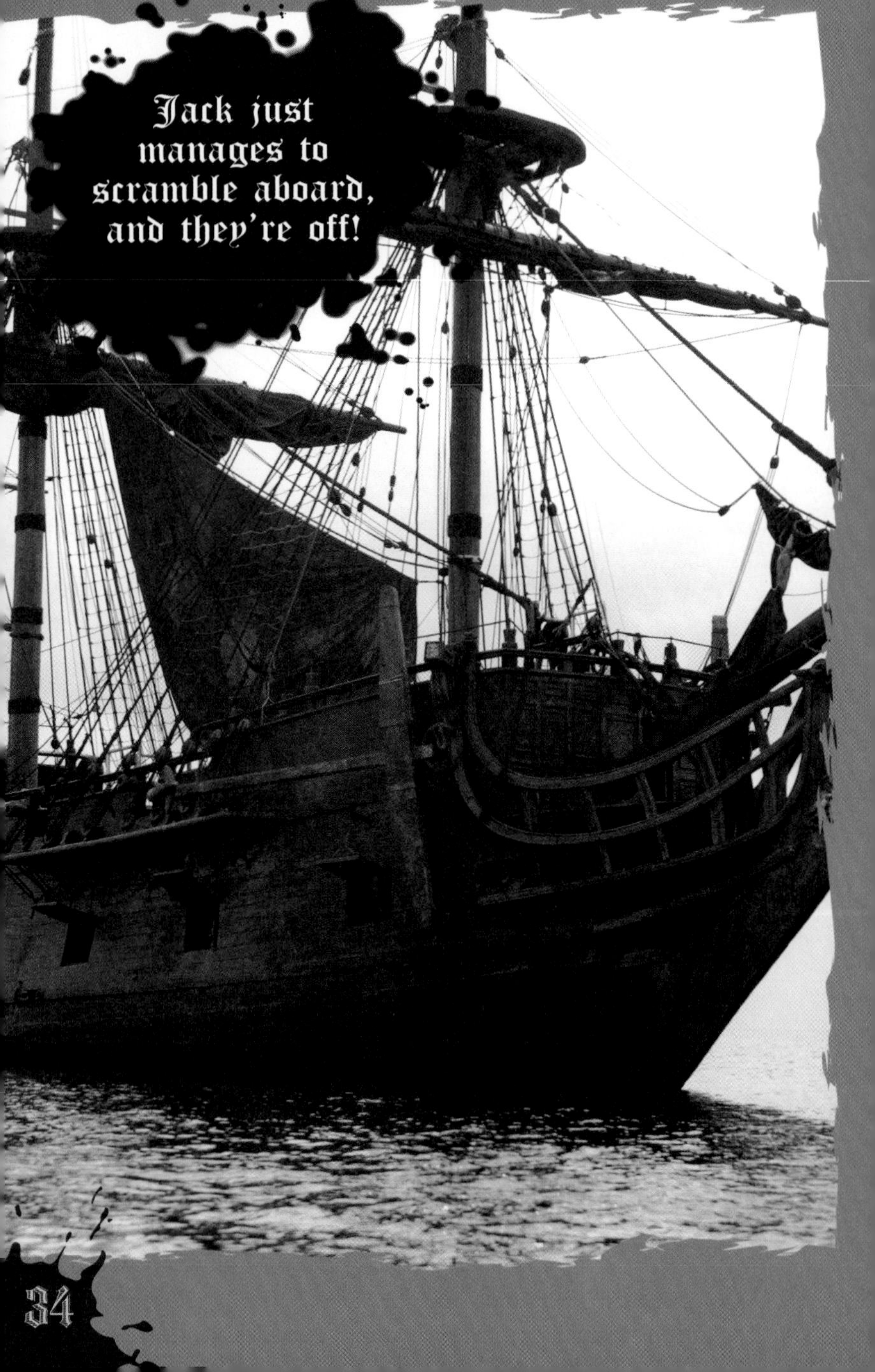

SETTINGS, CAPTAIN?
GO ANYWHERE, EXCEPT WHERE IT MIGHT MAKE SENSE FOR US TO GO.
The End... for now!

More Scenes from

DISNEY
PIRATES of the **CARIBBEAN**
DEAD MAN'S CHEST

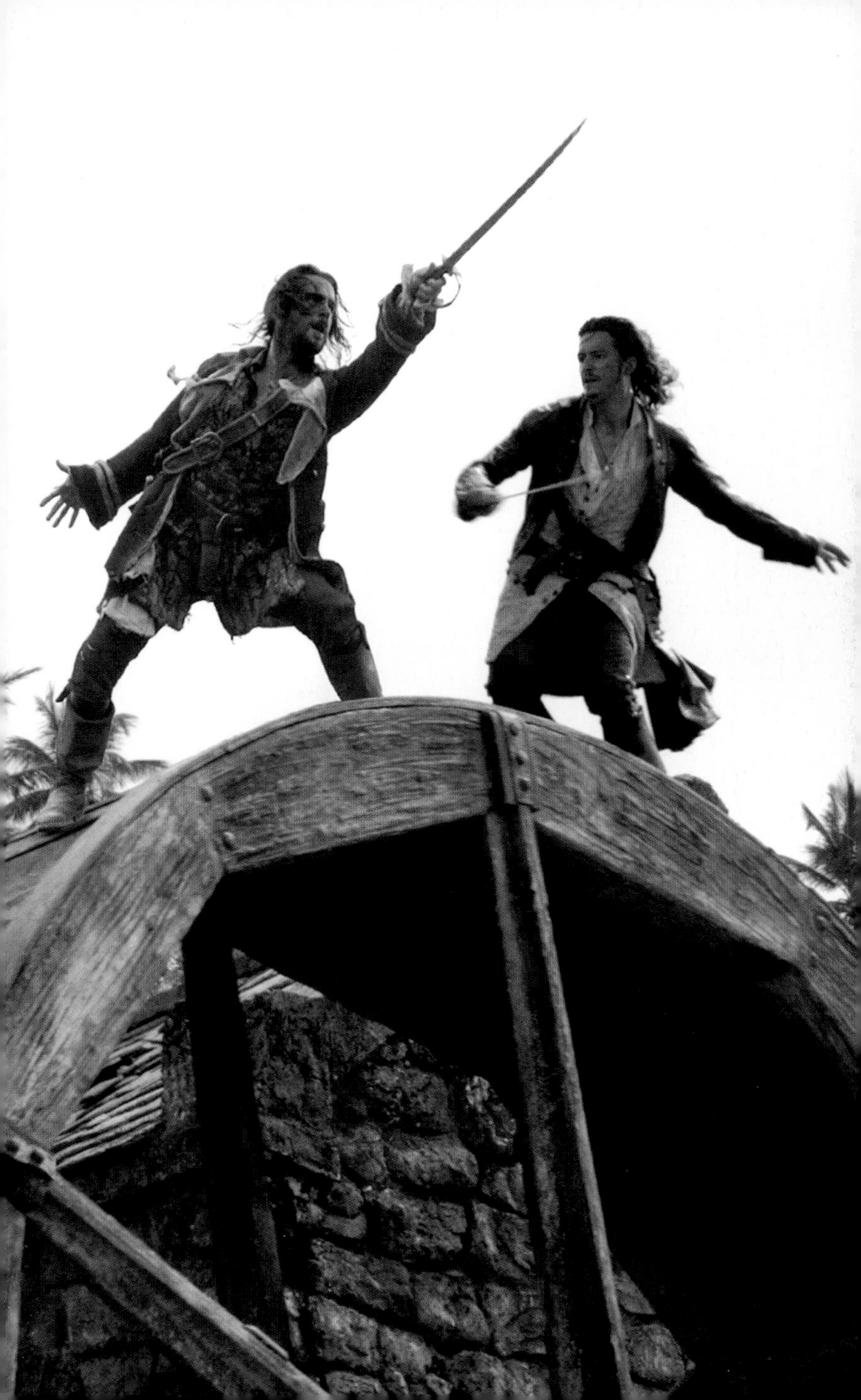

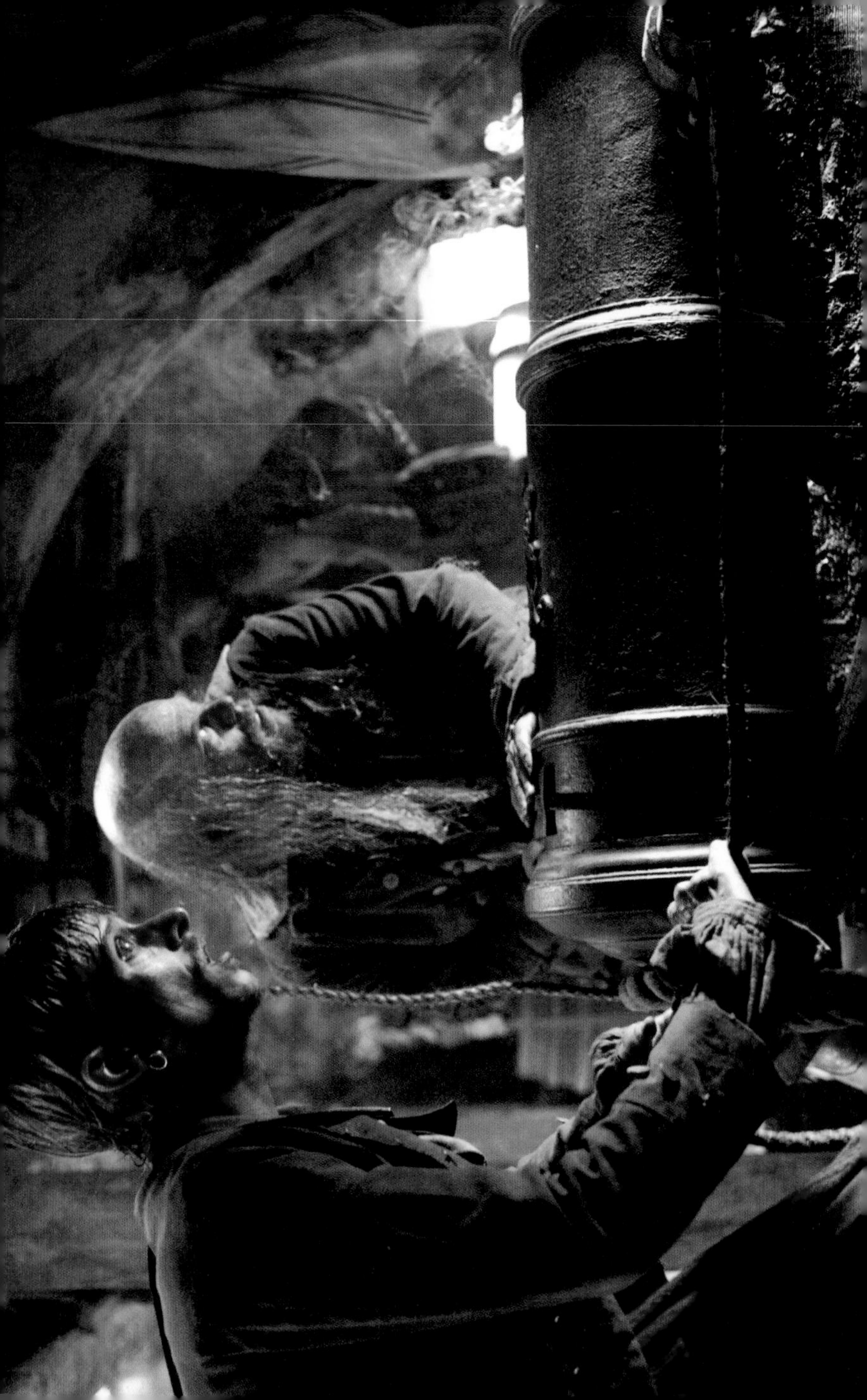

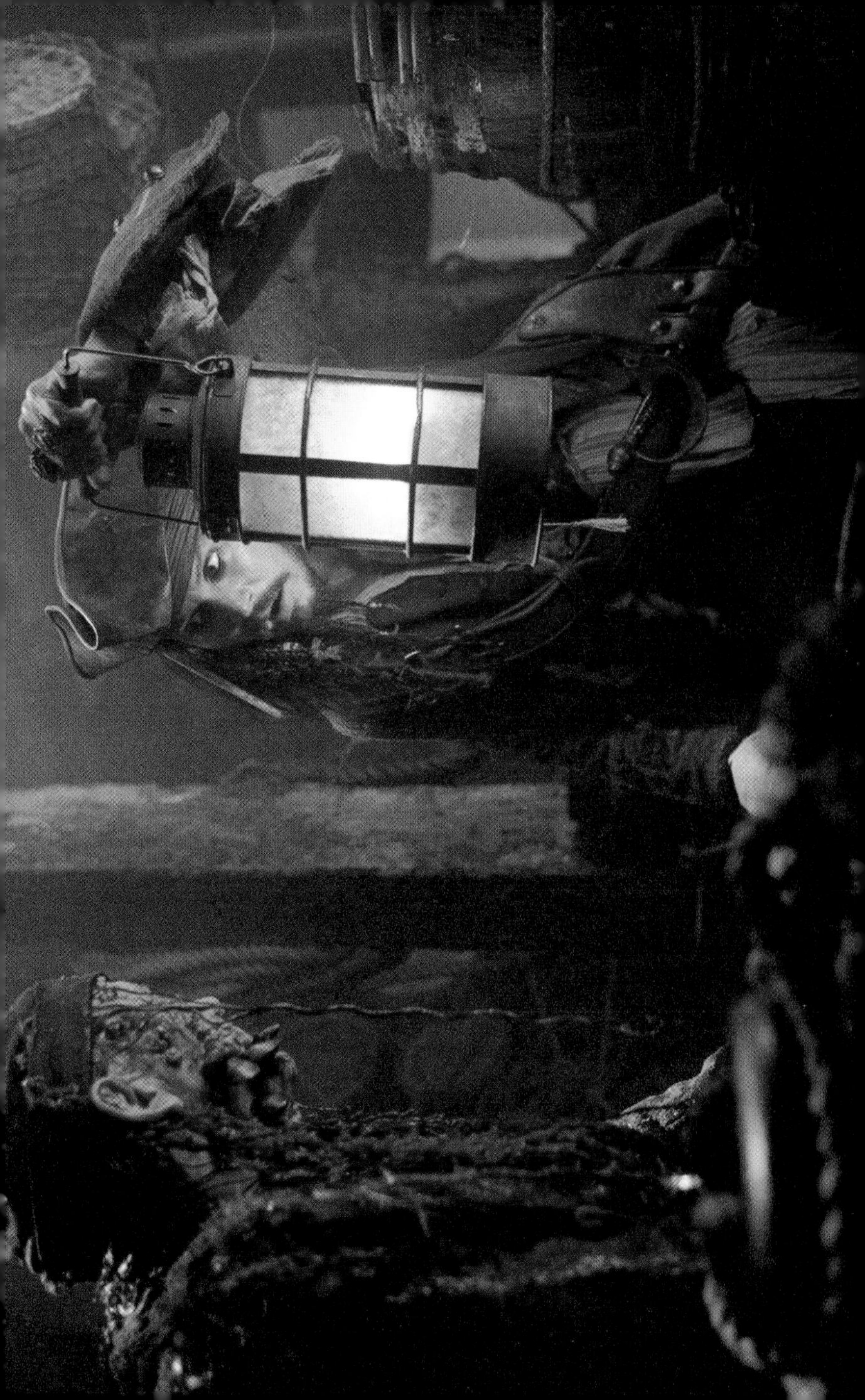

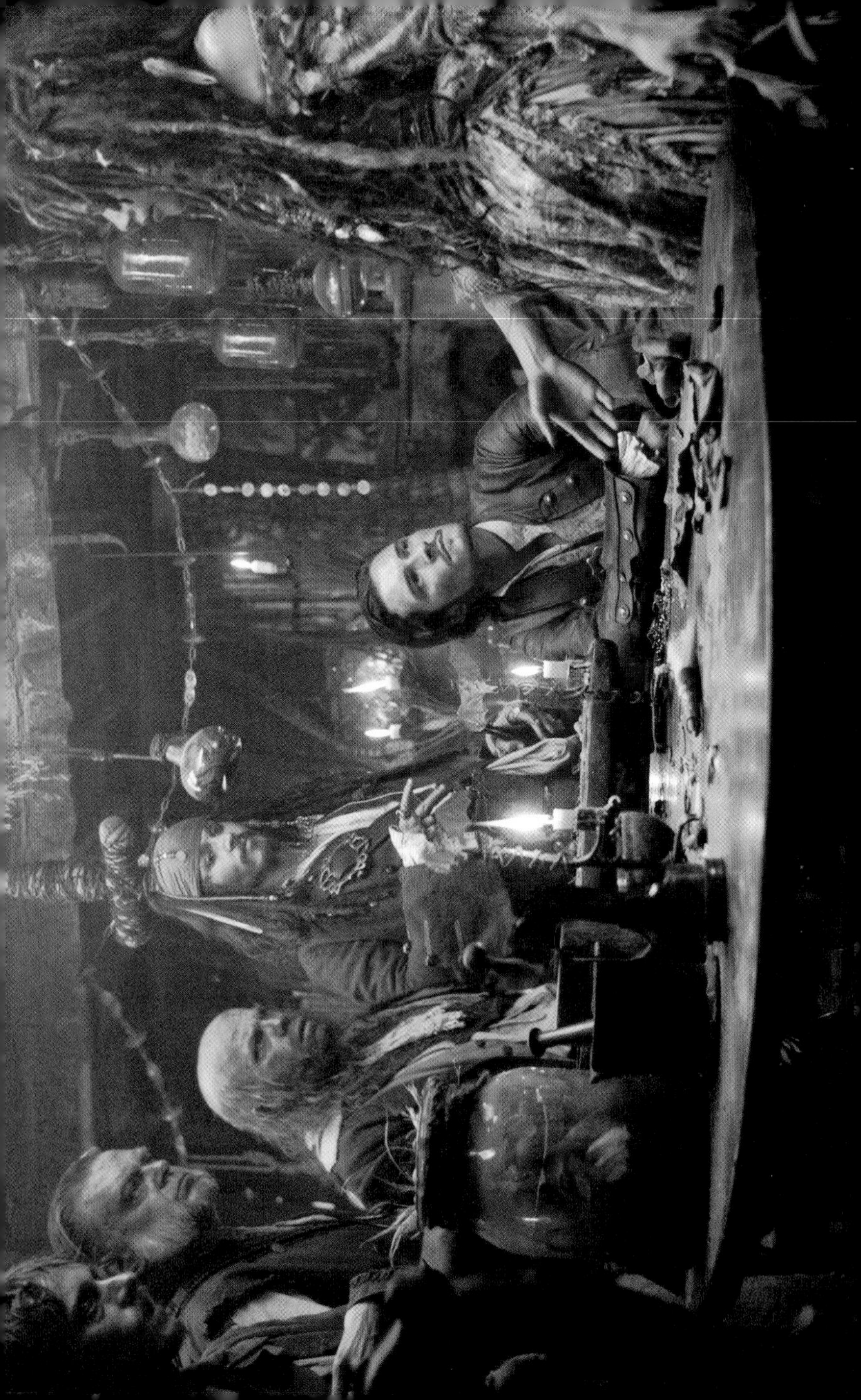

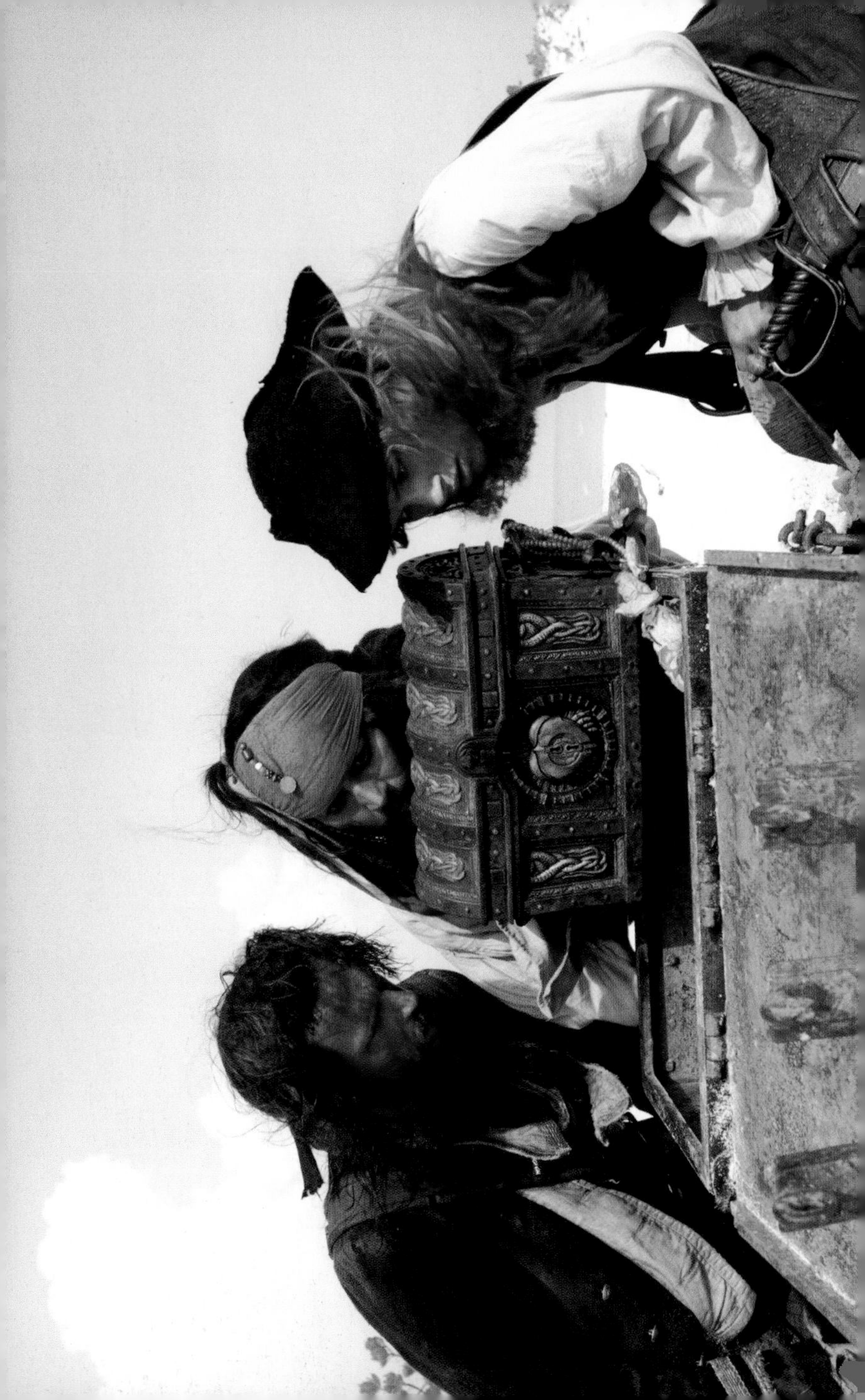

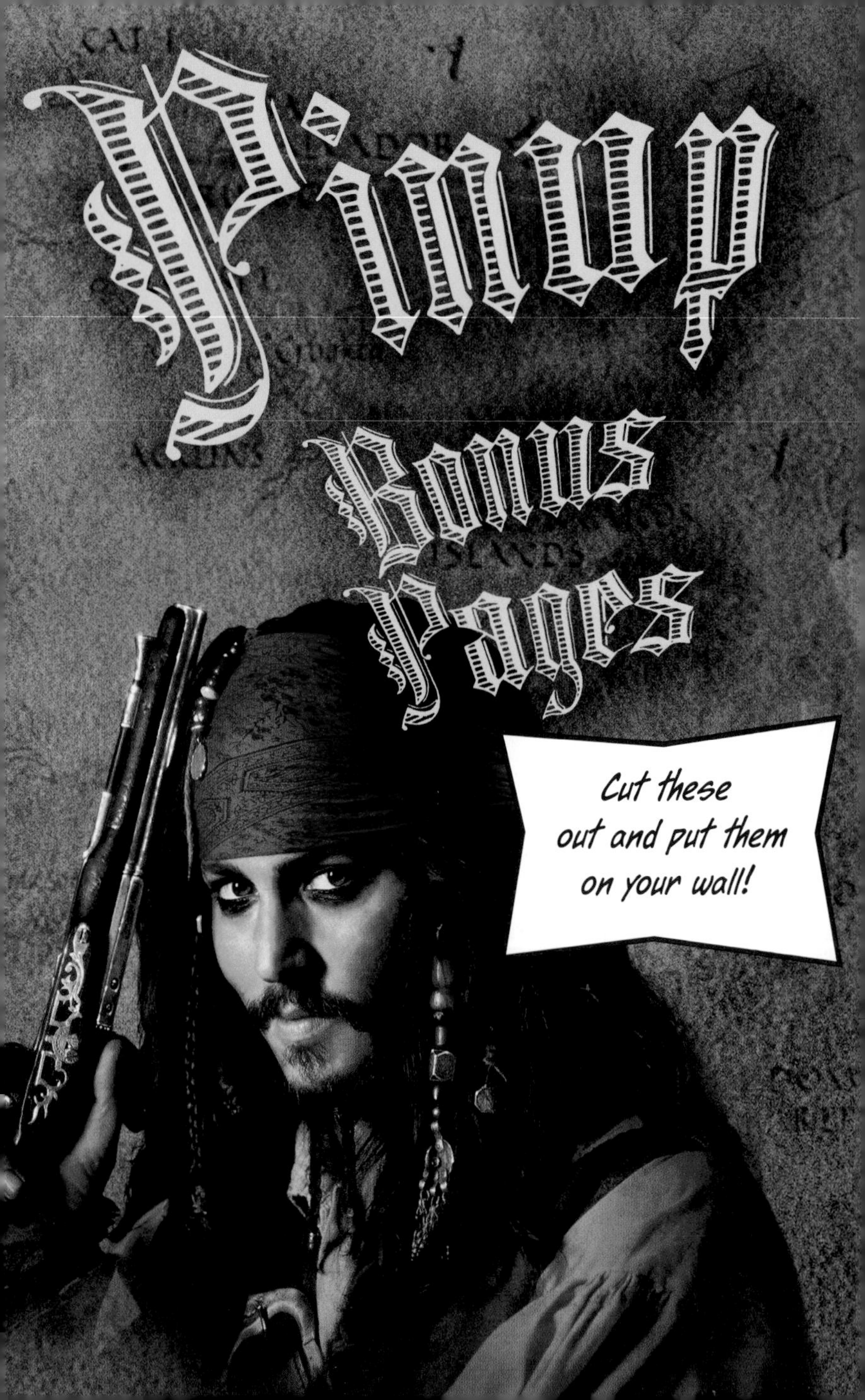
Pinup
Bonus
Pages
Cut these out and put them on your wall!

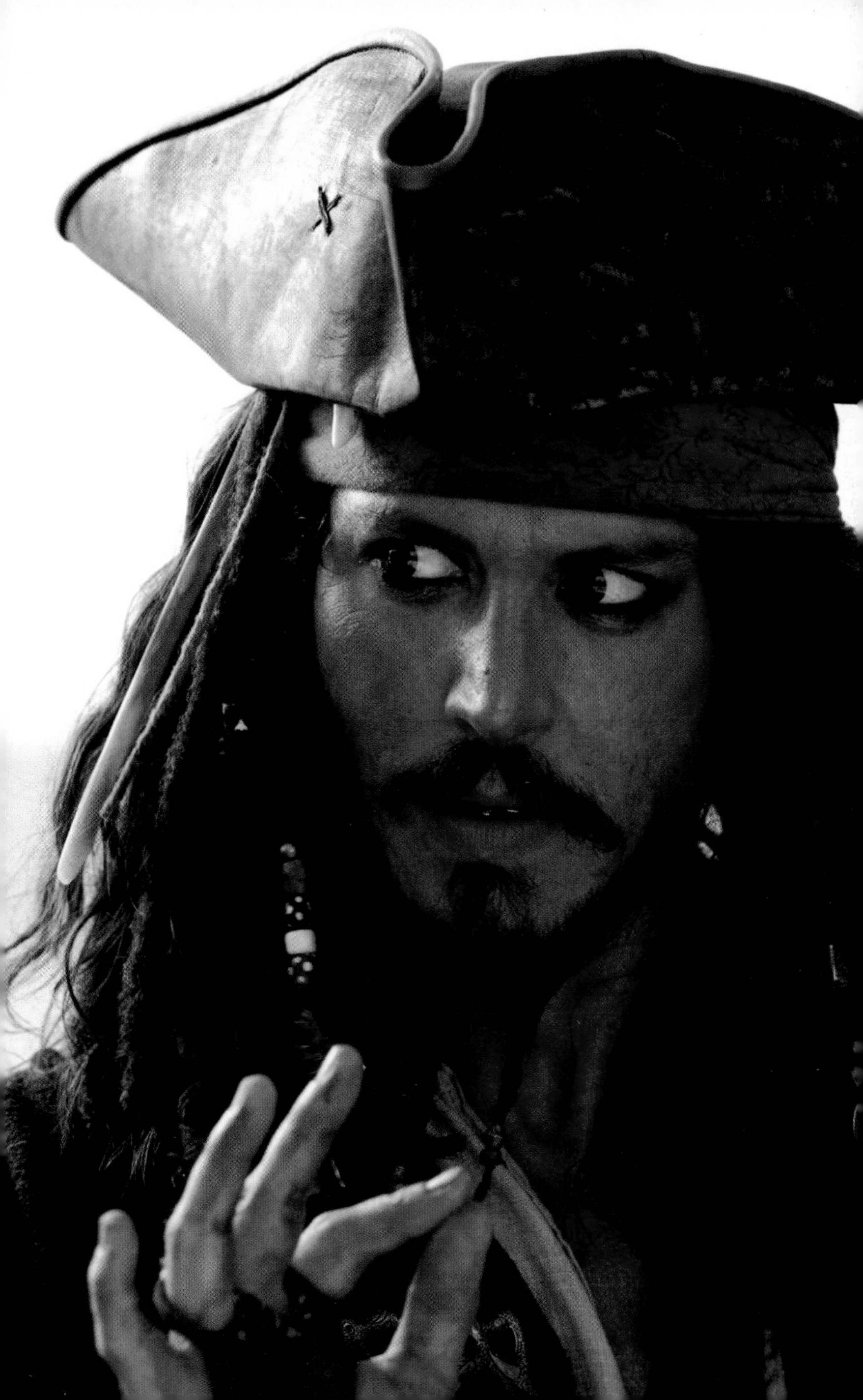

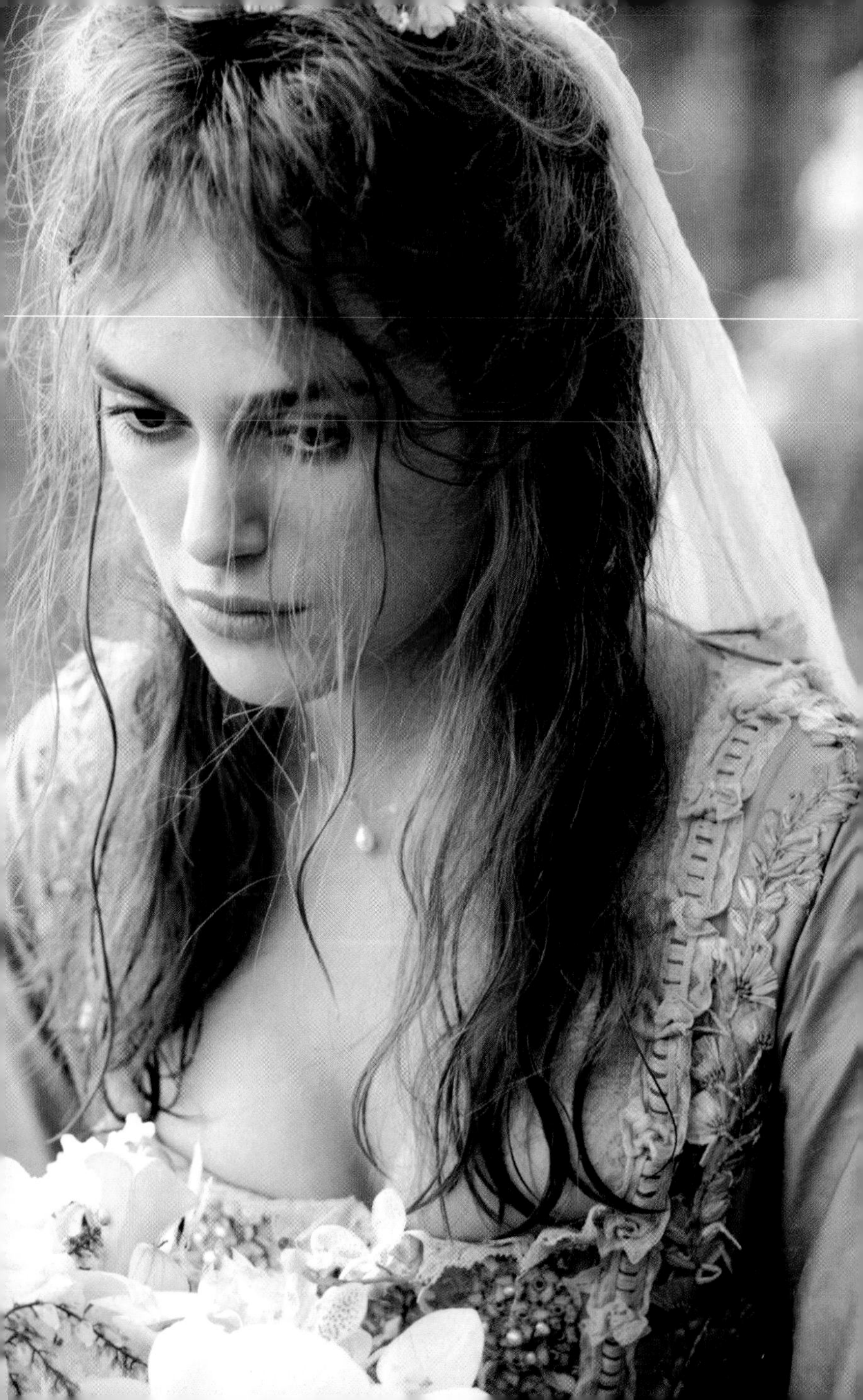

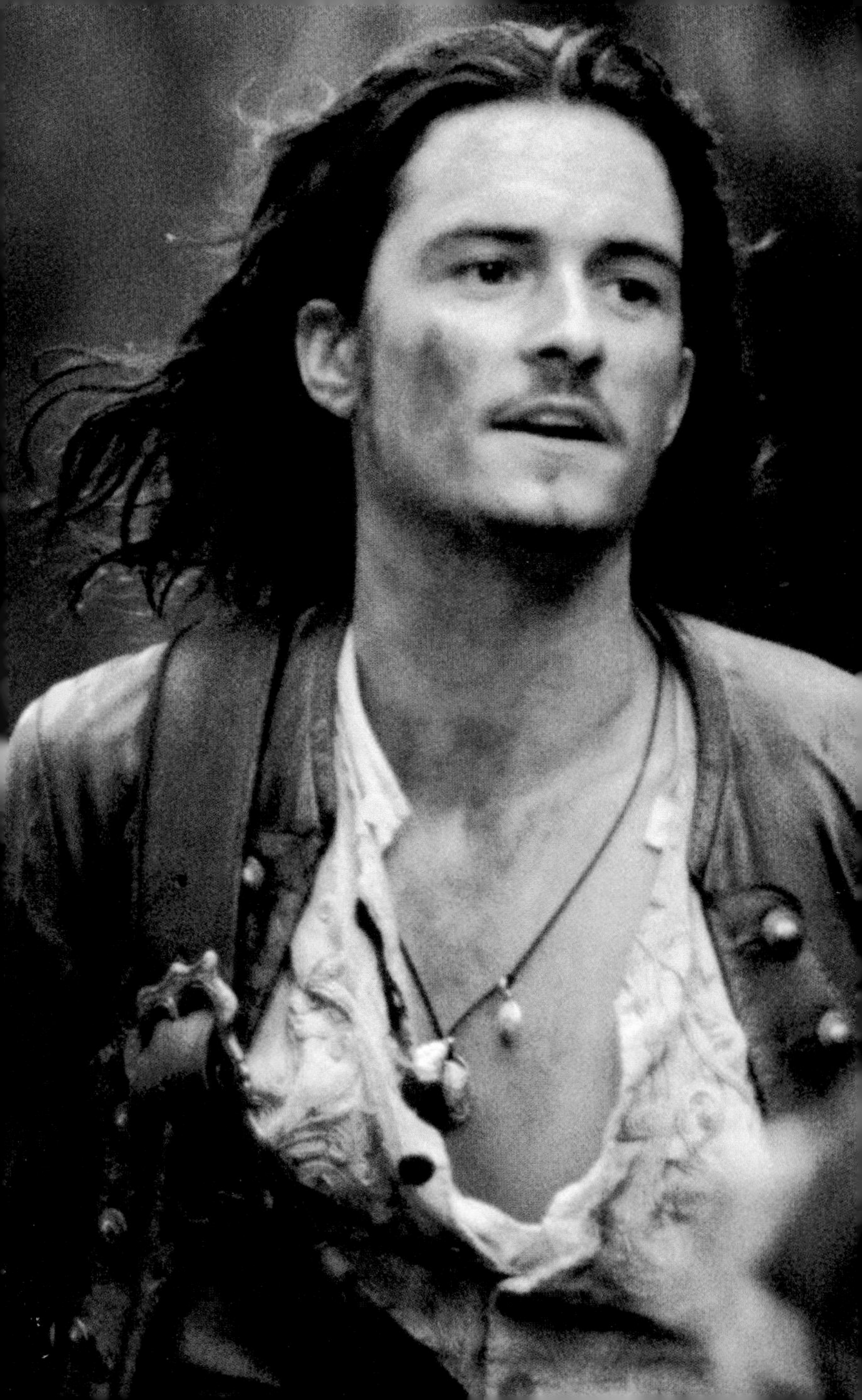

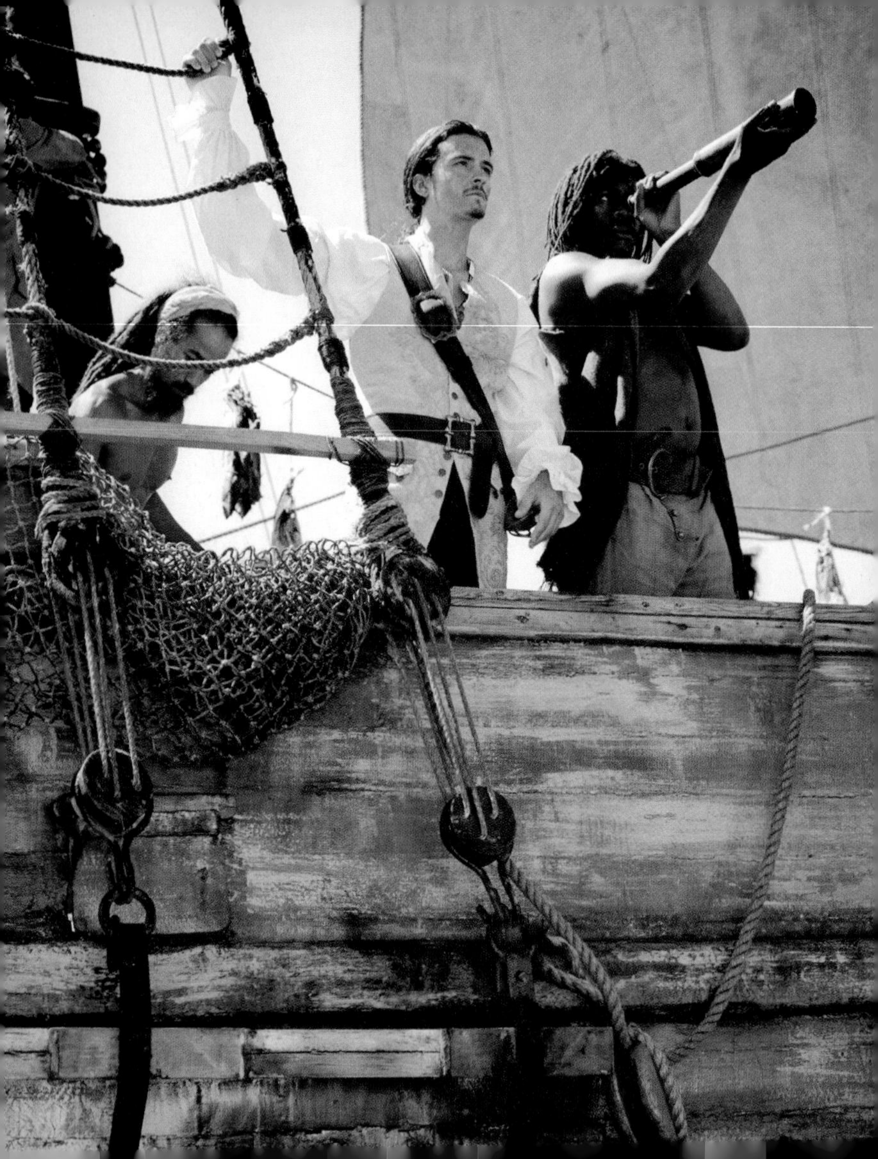

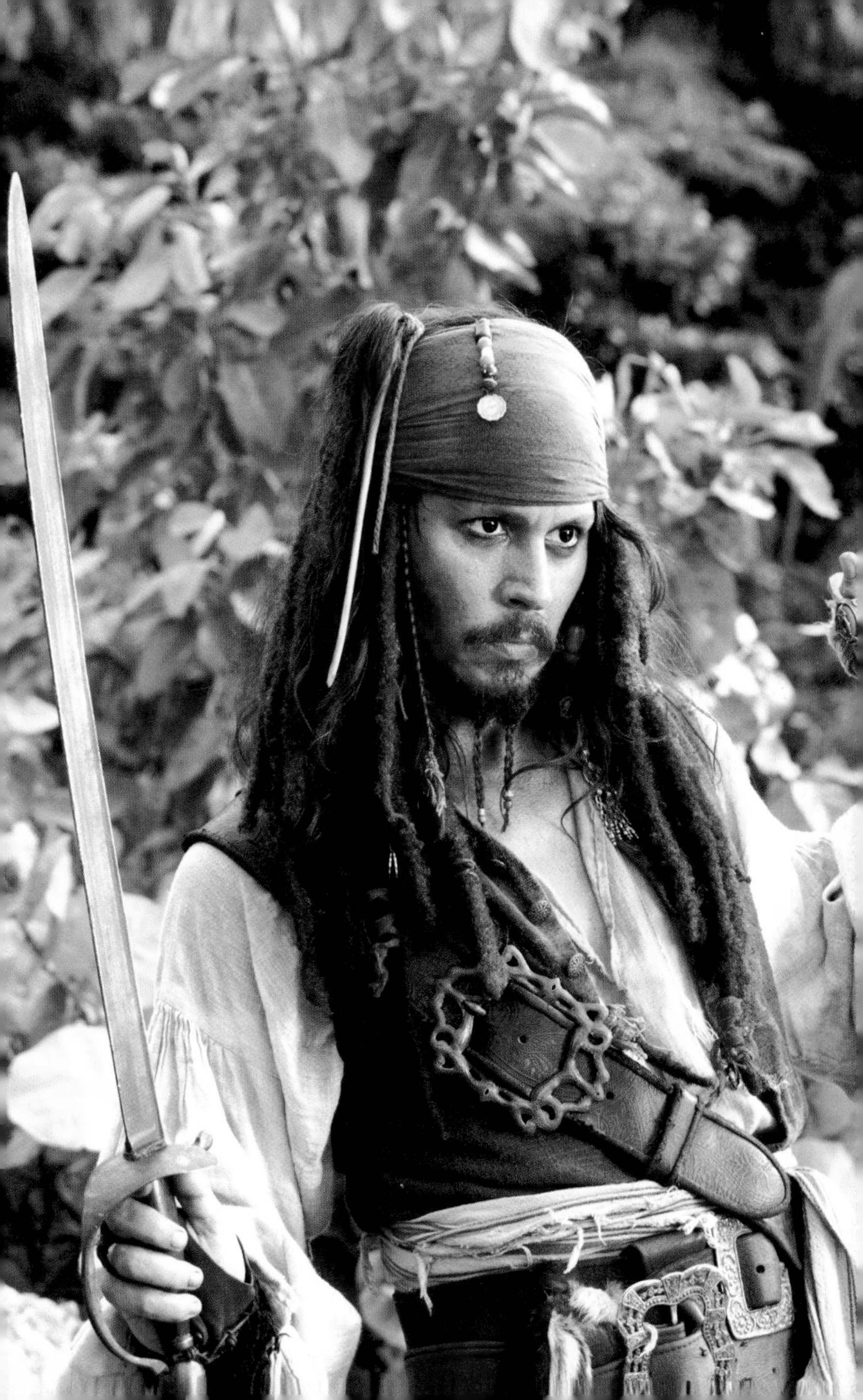

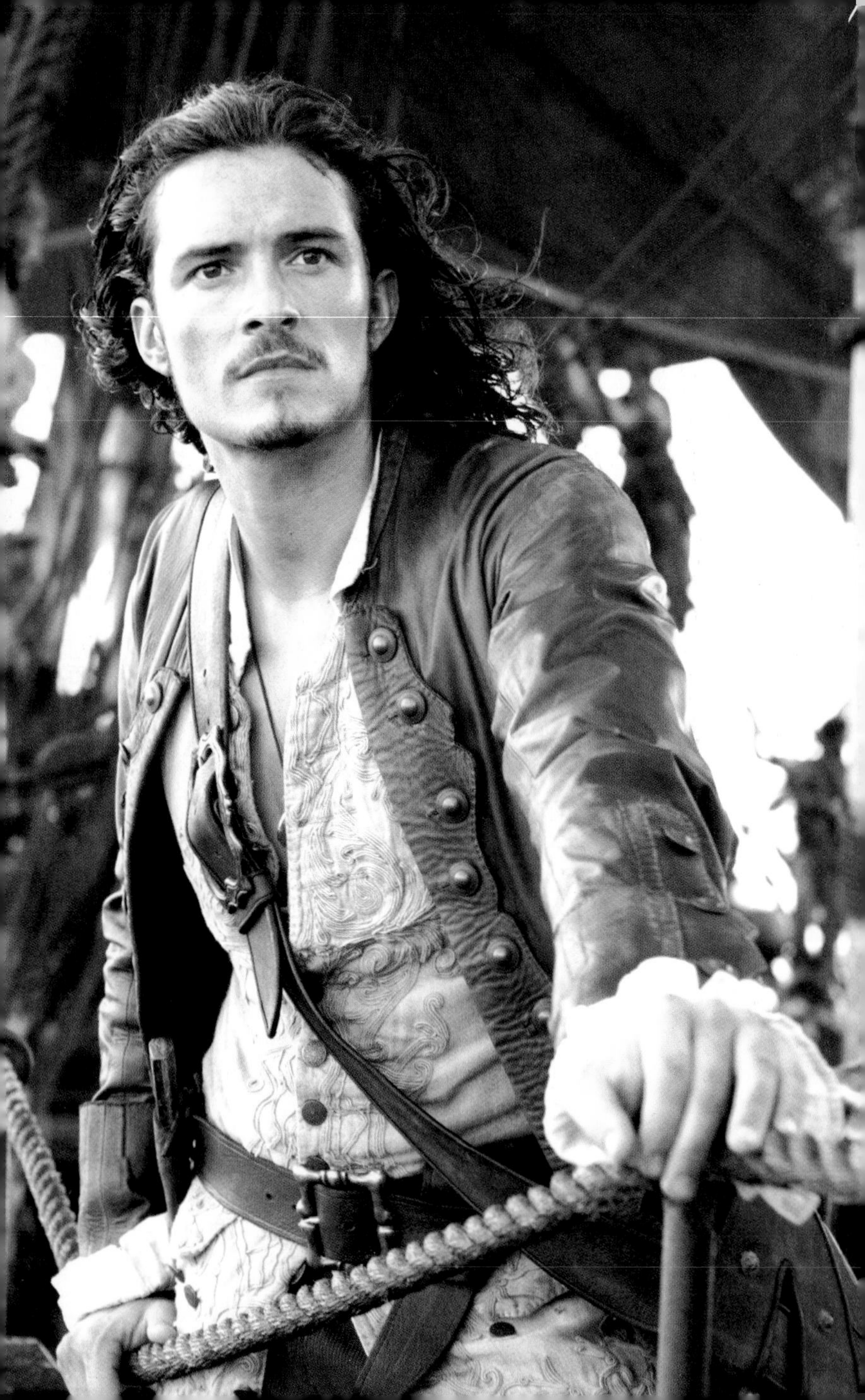